DOVER · THRIFT · EDITIONS

The Imaginary Invalid

MOLIÈRE

Translated by
Henri van Laun

❧

DOVER PUBLICATIONS, INC.
Mineola, New York

DOVER THRIFT EDITIONS

GENERAL EDITOR: PAUL NEGRI
EDITOR OF THIS VOLUME: JENNY BAK

Bibliographical Note

This Dover edition, first published in 2004, contains the unabridged text of *The Imaginary Invalid*, translated from the French by Henri van Laun, and originally published in volume III of *The Dramatic Works of Molière*, A. W. Lovering, Publisher, New York, 1875–1899. The introductory Note was prepared especially for this edition.

Library of Congress Cataloging-in-Publication Data

Molière, 1622-1673.
  [Malade imaginaire. English]
  The imaginary invalid / Molière ; translated by Henri Van Laun.
    p. cm. — (Dover thrift editions)
  ISBN-13: 0-486-43789-7 (pbk.)
  ISBN-10: 0-486-43789-2 (pbk.)
    1. Van Laun, Henri, 1820–1896. II. Title. III. Series.
PQ1835.A478 2004
842'.4—dc22

                                                                    2004049310

Manufactured in the United States by Courier Corporation
43789203   2013
www.doverpublications.com

Note

"MOLIÈRE" was the pseudonym of the French actor-manager and dramatist Jean Baptiste Poquelin (1622–1673). Born in Paris and educated at the Jesuit College de Cermont, Molière abandoned his studies in law and the prospect of a court appointment to form the company of L'Illustre Théâtre in 1643. The troupe, composed of Molière and members of the Bejard family, was not particularly successful during its two years in the capital—a time when Molière was imprisoned for non-payment of debts—and began touring the French provinces in 1645. During the next dozen or so years, Molière developed his theatrical skills to a high degree. He brought his polished theatrical company to Paris in 1658 and performed regularly before enthusiastic audiences. Among the troupe's devotees was King Louis XIV, who eventually became a close friend to Molière and godfather to his child. After a series of successful runs at the Petit-Bourbon, the company moved to the Palais-Royal in 1661, and was appointed the Troupe du roi in 1665.

Though his satirical works routinely angered influential members of church and state, Molière nevertheless found commercial success with such plays as *Tartuffe* and *Don Juan,* and critical acclaim with *The Misanthrope*. He was at the height of his commercial popularity when he penned his last work, *The Imaginary Invalid,* in late 1672. Written while suffering from a chronic respiratory infection, this comedy—an incisive satire of the medical profession—also mocked what the playwright perceived as mankind's excessive fear of death, as well as the paradoxical pleasure derived from believing oneself ill. Replete with fantastic interludes of music and dance, the work plays upon the dangers of the human imagination and its ability to override logic and common sense. The skewering of physicians and their dubious seventeenth-century knowledge (which was based largely on superstition and medieval practices) is clearly a response to Molière's personal encounters with them during his illness, and he justly parodies his own anxieties in the antics of the hypochondriacal title character, a role which he wrote for himself. Ironically, the lively comedy opened at the Palais-Royal during his final days. Weakened by a heavy cough, Molière collapsed during the play's fourth performance and succumbed to his illness later that night, on February 17, 1673.

LE MALADE IMAGINAIRE.

COMÉDIE.

THE IMAGINARY INVALID

A COMEDY IN THREE ACTS.

INTERSPERSED WITH MUSIC AND DANCING.

(*THE ORIGINAL IN PROSE.*)

FEBRUARY 10TH, 1673.

PROLOGUE.

After the glorious fatigues and the victorious exploits of our august monarch, it is quite right that those who write should labour either to praise or to amuse him. That is what we have wished to do here ; and this prologue is an attempt to praise this grand prince, which serves to introduce the comedy of *The Imaginary Invalid*, of which the purpose was to give him relief from his noble works.

DRAMATIS PERSONÆ.

IN THE COMEDY.

ARGAN, *an imaginary invalid.*[2]
BERALDE, *his brother.*[3]
CLEANTE, *Angelique's lover.*[4]
MR. PURGON, *Argan's physician.*
MR. DIAFOIRUS, *a physician.*
THOMAS DIAFOIRUS, *his son, betrothed to Angelique.*[5]

MR. FLEURANT, *an apothecary.*[6]
MR. DE BONNEFOI, *a notary.*
BELINE, *Argan's second wife.*
ANGELIQUE, *Argan's daughter.*
LOUISON (*a little girl*), *Argan's daughter.*
TOINETTE, *a servant.*

IN THE PROLOGUE.

FLORA. TWO DANCING ZEPHYRS. CLIMENE. DAPHNE.
TIRCIS, *Climene's lover, chief of a troop of shepherds.*
DORILAS, *Daphne's lover, chief of a troop of shepherds.*
SHEPHERDS *and* SHEPHERDESSES *of the suite of Tircis.*
SHEPHERDS *and* SHEPHERDESSES *of the suite of Dorilas.*
PAN.
FAUNS (*dancing*).

IN THE INTERLUDES.

First Act.

PUNCH.   AN OLD WOMAN.   VIOLIN-PLAYERS.
        ARCHERS (*dancing and singing*).

Second Act.

FOUR SINGING GIPSIES.   OTHER SINGING AND DANCING GIPSIES.

Third Act.

SINGING UPHOLSTERERS.
THE PRESIDENT OF THE MEDICAL FACULTY.
PHYSICIANS.
ARGAN.

BACHELOR.
APOTHECARIES (*with their mortars and pestles*).
SURGEONS.
SYRINGE-BEARERS.

Scene.—PARIS.

---

[2] This part was played by Molière. According to the description of the dresses given in the first surreptitious publication of this comedy, by Daniel Elzevir, Amsterdam, 1674, "Argan was arrayed as an invalid, coarse stockings, slippers, a tight pair of breeches, a red waistcoat with some embroidery or lace, a neckerchief with old lace negligently fastened, a night-cap with a lace skull-cap."

[3] Dressed as a modest cavalier.

[4] Dressed as a gallant and a lover.

[5] Mr. Diafoirus, his son, and Mr. Purgon are all dressed in black; the first two as ordinary physicians, and the last with a large smooth collar, having long sleek hair, and a cloak coming below his knees.

[6] He is also dressed in black or brownish grey, with a short apron, and a clyster in his hand, without a hat.

THE IMAGINARY INVALID.

(*LE MALADE IMAGINAIRE*).

ECLOGUE WITH MUSIC AND DANCING.
The Scene represents a rustic, pleasant spot.

Scene I.—Flora, Two Zephyrs, dancing.

FLO.   Leave, leave your flocks ;
Come shepherds, shepherdesses all ;
Assemble 'neath these youthful elms :
I have come to announce to you sweet tidings,
Wherewith these hamlets to rejoice.
Leave, leave your flocks ;
Come shepherds, shepherdesses all ;
Assemble 'neath these youthful elms.

Scene II.—Flora, Two Zephyrs dancing ; Climène,
Daphné, Tircis, Dorilas.

CLI. (*To Tircis*).   DAPH. (*To Dorilas*).
Leave your protestations, shepherd :
It is Flora who now calls.

TIR. (*To Climène*).   DOR. (*To Daphné*).
But cruel one, tell me at least,
If by a little friendship, you will repay my vows.
TIR. If you will be sensible of my faithful ardour.
CLI. AND DAPH. It is Flora who now calls.

1

TIR. AND DOR. It is but a word, a word, a word only that I crave.

TIR. Shall I for ever languish in my mortal pain?

DOR. May I hope that one day you shall make me happy?

CLI. AND DAPH. It is Flora who now calls.

Scene III.— Flora, Two Zephyrs dancing; Climène, Daphné, Tircis, Dorilas, Shepherds and Shepherdesses, of the suite of Tircis and Dorilas, dancing and singing.

First Entry of the Ballet.

All the Shepherds and Shepherdesses place themselves around Flora, keeping time to the music.

CLI.   What news is that, O goddess,
              That amongst us is to diffuse so much joy?

DAPH.   We burn to learn from you,
              These important tidings.

DOR.   Eagerly we all sigh for it.

CLI., DAPH., TIR., DOR.
              With impatience we die for it.

FLO.   Here it is; silence, silence,
              Your prayers have been granted, Louis is
                  returned;
              In these spots he brings back pleasures and
                  love,
              And you behold an end to your mortal alarms.
              By his vast exploits, he sees everything sub-
                  jected:
                      He lays down his arms,
                      Failing foes.

CHORUS.   Ah! what sweet news!
              How grand it is, how beautiful it is!
              What pleasure! what laughter! what sports!
                  what happy successes!
              And how well Heaven has fulfilled our wishes!
              Ah! what sweet news!
              How grand it is! how beautiful it is!

Second Entry of the Ballet.

*All the Shepherds and Shepherdesses express by their dances,
the transports of their joy.*

FLO.   From your rural pipes
    Evoke the sweetest sounds ;
    Louis offers to your songs
    The most be autiful subject.
    After a hundred battles,
    In which his arm
    Reaps an ample victory,
    Form amongst you
    A hundred battles still more sweet,
    To sing his glory.

CHORUS. Let us form amongst us
    A hundred battles still more sweet,
    To sing his glory.

FLO.   My youthful lover, in these woods,
    From my empire prepares a present,
    As a prize for the voice
    Who shall best succeed in telling us
    The virtue and the exploits
    Of the most august of kings.

CLI. If Tircis has the advantage.
DAPH. If Dorilas conqueror be.
CLI. To cherish him I promise.
DAPH. To his ardour I will give myself.
TIR. Oh hope too dear !
DOR. Oh word replete with sweetness !
TIR. AND DOR. Could grander subject, sweeter reward
animate a heart ?

*The violins play an air to animate the two shepherds to the
competition, while Flora, as umpire, places herself, with two
Zephyrs, at the foot of a beautiful tree in the middle of the
stage, and the rest occupy the two sides, as spectators.*

TIR. When the melted snow swells a famous torrent,
   Against the sudden effort of its frothy waves
   There is nothing sufficiently solid ;
   Dykes, castles, towns, and woods,

Men and flocks at one and the same time,
All things bend to the current which guides it:
Such, and fiercer, and more rapid still
Louis marches in his exploits.

Third Entry of the Ballet.

The Shepherds and Shepherdesses at Tircis' side dance round him, to the measure of a ritornello, to express their applause.

DOR. The threatening lightning that with fury pierces
The horrible darkness, by a fiery glow,
Causes, with fear and terror,
The most steadfast heart to tremble ;
But, at the head of an army,
Louis inspires more terror still.

Fourth Entry of the Ballet.

The Shepherds and Shepherdesses at Dorilas' side do the same thing as the others have done.

TIR. We see the fabulous exploits which Greece has sung,
Effaced by many grander truths ;
And all these famous demi-gods
Whom past history vaunts,
Are not even to our thoughts
What Louis is in our eyes.

Fifth Entry of the Ballet.

The Shepherds and Shepherdesses once more do the same thing that the others have done.

DOR. In our days, Louis, by his astonishing feats,
Makes us believe the grand deeds which history has sung
Of by-gone ages ;
But our nephews, in their glory,
Shall have nothing that can make believe
All the grand feats of Louis.

Sixth Entry of the Ballet.

The Shepherds and Shepherdesses at Dorilas' side again do the same things.

Seventh Entry of the Ballet.

The Shepherds and Shepherdesses on both sides mingle and dance together.

Scene VI.—*Flora, Pan; Two Zephyrs dancing; Climène, Daphné, Tircis, Dorilas, Fauns dancing, Shepherds and Shepherdesses dancing and singing.*

PAN. Abandon, abandon, shepherds, this bold design,
    Eh ! what would you do?
    Sing on your pipes
    What Apollo, on his lyre,
    With his most lovely songs,
    Would not undertake to say?
    It is giving too much flight to the fire that inspires
        you,
    It is mounting towards the sky on waxen wings,
    To drop down to the bottom of the deep,
    To sing the intrepid courage of Louis,
    There is no voice that is learned enough,
    There are no words grand enough to describe it ;
    Silence is the language
    That must laud his exploits.
    Consecrate other cares to his signal victory ;
    Your praises have naught that flatters his desires:
    Leave, leave his glory ;
    Think of nothing but his pleasures.

CHOR. Leave, leave his glory ;
    Think of nothing but his pleasures.

FLO. (*To Tircis and to Dorilas*).
    Although, to laud his immortal virtues,
    Strength may fail your minds,
    Both may receive the prize.
    In grand and beauteous things
    It is sufficient to have tried.

Eighth Entry of the Ballet.

The two Zephyrs dance with two chaplets of flowers in their hands, which they afterwards give to the two Shepherds.

CLI. AND DAPH. (*Giving their lovers their hands*).
        In grand and beauteous things,
        It is sufficient to have tried.

TIR. AND DOR. Ah! with what sweet rewards our bold-
ness has been crowned!

FLO. AND PAN. What one does for Louis is never lost.

CLI., DAPH., TIR., DOR.

Let us give ourselves henceforth to the
care for his pleasures.

FLO. AND PAN. Happy, happy, who can devote his life
to him!

CHORUS. In these woods let us mingle
Our flutes and our voices;
This day invites us to it.
And let us make the echoes resound a thou-
sand times,
Louis is the greatest of kings,
Happy, happy who can devote his life to him!

Ninth Entry of the Ballet.

*Fauns, Shepherds, and Shepherdesses all mingle together to
execute a dance; after which they go to prepare
themselves for the Comedy.*

ANOTHER PROLOGUE.[7]

SCENE I.—*A Shepherdess singing.*

Your highest knowledge is but pure chimera,
Vain and not very learned doctors;
You cannot cure, by your grand Latin words,
The grief that causes my despair.
Your highest knowledge is but pure chimera.

---

[7] This second prologue is not in the libretto of the ballet. It was pro-
ably often used, both for shortness' sake, and because it announces the
subject of the Comedy, and is to be found in the Amsterdam edition. It
is preceded by the following description :—
The theatre represents a forest. When the stage is seen, an agreeable
noise of instruments is heard. Afterwards, a Shepherdess comes to complain tenderly that she finds no remedy for the pangs which she suffers.
Several Fauns and Ægyptians, assembled for their peculiar festival and
games, meet the Shepherdess. They listen to her complaints, and form
a very amusing spectacle. Complaint of the Shepherdess :—

Alas ! alas ! I dare not reveal
    My love-sick martyrdom
To the shepherd for whom I sigh,
And who alone can relieve me.
Do not pretend to put an end to it,
    Ignorant doctors, you would not know how to do it :
Your highest knowledge is but pure chimera.

These uncertain remedies, of which the simple people
Think that you know the admirable virtue,
Cannot cure the ills I feel :
And all your gibberish can be received
    Only by an *Imaginary Invalid.*
Your highest knowledge is but pure chimera,
    Vain and little informed doctors, etc.

The Scene changes, and represents an apartment.

_____

ACT I.

SCENE I.—ARGAN, *seated before a table, is adding up his
apothecary's bill with counters.*

AR. Three and two make five, and five make ten, and
ten make twenty ; three and two make five. "Besides,
on the twenty-fourth,[8] a small clyster, mild, preparative
and soothing, to soothe, moisten, and refresh Mr. Argan's
inward parts." What pleases me in Mr. Fleurant, my
apothecary, is that his bills are always so civil. "Mr.
Argan's inward parts, thirty sols." Yes ; but, Mr. Fleurant, to be civil is not everything ; you should also be
moderate, and not flay your patients. Thirty sols an
enema ! I am your humble servant, I have already told
you ; in your other bills you have put them at only twenty
sols ; and twenty sols in apothecary's language means ten
sols ; here they are, ten sols. "Besides, on the said date,
a good cleaning clyster, composed of double catholicon,
rhubarb, with honey of roses, and other ingredients,

_____

[8] As Argan's verification of medicine delivered during the entire month
would be too long, the curtain rises when he is at the twenty-fourth day.

according to prescription, to scour, wash and clean the lower abdomen of Mr. Argan, thirty sols." By your leave, ten sols. "Besides, on the said date, in the evening, a julep for the liver, soporative and soporific, composed to make Mr. Argan sleep, thirty-five sols." I do not complain of this, for it made me sleep very well. Ten, fifteen, sixteen, and seventeen sols, six deniers.[9] "Besides, on the twenty-fifth, a good purgative and strengthening draught, composed of fresh cassia, with Levantine senna, and other ingredients, according to the prescription of Mr. Purgon, to expel and evacuate Mr. Argan's bile, four francs." Ah! Mr. Fleurant, this is too much of a joke: one should give and take with patients. Mr. Purgon did not order you to put down four francs. Put down, put down three francs, if you please. Twenty and thirty sols.[10] "Besides, on the same date, an anodyne and astringent potion, to procure Mr. Argan some rest, thirty sols." Good, ten and fifteen sols.[11] "Besides, on the twenty-sixth, a carminative clyster, to drive away Mr. Argan's flatulence, thirty sols." Ten sols, Mr. Fleurant. "Besides the same clyster, repeated in the evening, as above, thirty sols." Mr. Fleurant, ten sols. "Besides, on the twenty-seventh, a good draught to hasten and drive out the bad humours of Mr. Argan, three livres." Good, twenty and thirty sols; I am glad that you are reasonable. "Besides, on the twenty-eighth, a small dose of clarified and edulcorated milk, to soften, temper, refresh, and purify Mr. Argan's blood, twenty sols." Good, ten sols.[12] Besides, a cordial and preservative potion, composed of twelve grains of bezoar, syrup of lemon and pomegranates, and other ingredients, according to prescription, five livres." Ah! Mr. Fleurant, gently if you please, if you go on thus, one would no longer care to be ill: be satisfied with four francs; twenty and forty sols. Three and two make

---

[9] Argan always puts down half of what the apothecary asks. Although the julep has done him good, he puts down only seventeen sous, six deniers,—half of Mr. Fleurant's charge, which was thirty-five sous.

[10] Here Argan puts down again the half of the three francs, the apothecary's charge, and says "thirty sols." He first marks with his counters twenty sols, and then adds ten more, which make thirty, but never thought of putting down fifty.

[11] See note above.   [12] See note above.

five, and five make ten, and ten make twenty. Sixty-
three livres, four sols, and six deniers. So that, this
month, I have taken, one, two, three, four, five, six, seven
and eight remedies; and one, two, three, four, five, six,
seven, eight, nine, ten, eleven and twelve enemas; and
the other month, there were twelve remedies and twenty
enemas. I am not surprised that I am not so well this
month as the other. I had better tell this to Mr. Purgon,
so that he may set this matter to rights. Come, take all
this away. (*Seeing that no one comes, that there are none
of his servants in the room*). There is no one here. I
may say what I like, I am always left alone: there is no
means of making them stay here. (*After having rung a
bell that is on the table*). They do not hear, and my bell
does not make sufficient noise. Tingle, tingle, tingle.[13]
Not a bit of use. Tingle, tingle, tingle! They are
deaf. . . . Toinette! Tingle, tingle, tingle. Just as
if I did not ring at all. You wretch! you slut! Tingle,
tingle, tingle.[14] I am in a rage! Tingle, tingle, tingle!
To the devil with you, baggage! Is it possible that they
can leave a poor invalid by himself in this way? Tingle,
tingle, tingle. This is most wretched. Tingle, tingle,
tingle! Ah! good Heavens! they will leave me to die
here! tingle, tingle, tingle.

SCENE II.—ARGAN, TOINETTE.

TOI. (*Entering*). Coming, coming.

ARG. Ah! slut! ah! baggage . . .

TOI. (*Pretends to have knocked her head*). The deuce
take your impatience! You hurry people so, that I have
given myself a great knock on the head against the outside corner of the shutter.

ARG. (*Angry*). Ah! you wretch! . . .

TOI. (*Interrupting him*). Ah!

ARG. It is an . . .

TOI. Ah! . . .

ARG. It is an hour . . .

---

[13] In the original, *Drelin*, a word invented to imitate the sound of a bell
when rung.

[14] Argan no longer rings his bell, but shouts.

Toi. Ah!

Arg. That you have left me . . .

Toi. Ah!

Arg. Hold your tongue, you slut, that I may scold you.

Toi. Upon my word, I like that. I should advise you to do so, after what I have just done to myself.

Arg. You have given me a sore throat, you slut.

Toi. And you have given me a broken head : one is as good as the other. We are quits, if you like.

Arg. What! you baggage . . .

Toi. If you scold, I shall cry.

Arg. To leave me, you wretch . . .

Toi. (*Once more interrupting Argan*). Ah!

Arg. You slut! . . . you wish me to . . .

Toi. Ah!

Arg. What! I am not to have the pleasure of scolding her!

Toi. Scold as much as you like : I am agreeable.

Arg. You prevent me, you slut, by interrupting me at every point.

Toi. If you have the pleasure of scolding, I may, on my side, have the pleasure of crying : each his own ; that is not too much. Ah!

Arg. Come, I shall have to do without it. Take this away, you wretch, take this away. (*After having risen*). Has my enema of to-day acted well?

Toi. Your enema?

Arg. Yes. Had I much bile?

Toi. Upon my word, I do not meddle with these things, it is for Mr. Fleurant to put his nose into them, since he profits by them.

Arg. Let them take care to keep some beef-tea ready for me, for the other which I am to take by-and-bye.

Toi. This Mr. Fleurant, and this Mr. Purgon amuse themselves very much with your body; they have a good milch-cow in you ; and I should much like to ask them what disease you have, to want so many remedies.

Arg. Hold your tongue, you ignorant woman; it is not for you to control the prescriptions of the faculty. Send my daughter Angélique to me: I have something to say to her.

TOI. Here she comes of her own accord; she has guessed your thought.

SCENE III.—ARGAN, ANGÉLIQUE, TOINETTE.

ARG. Come here, Angélique: you come opportunely; I wished to speak to you.

AN. Behold me ready to listen to you.

ARG. Wait. (*To Toinette*). Give me my stick. I shall be back in a moment.

TOI. Go quickly, Sir, go. Mr. Fleurant gives us some work.

SCENE IV.—ANGÉLIQUE, TOINETTE.

AN. Toinette!

TOI. What!

AN. Just look at me.

TOI. Well! I am looking at you.

AN. Toinette!

TOI. Well! what, Toinette?

AN. Cannot you guess what I wish to speak about?

TOI. I have my doubts about it: of our young lover; for it is on him that for six days all our conversations turn; and you are not at your ease, unless you talk of him at every moment.

AN. Since you know that, why are you not the first to converse with me about it? And why do you not save me the trouble of dragging you into this conversation?

TOI. You do not give me time to do so; and you are so anxious about it, that it becomes difficult to forestall you.

AN. I confess to you that I cannot tire of speaking of him to you, and that my heart warmly takes advantage of every moment to open itself to you. But tell me, Toinette, do you condemn the sentiments which I have for him?

TOI. I have no such thoughts.

AN. Am I wrong in abandoning myself to these sweet impressions?

TOI. I do not say so.

AN. And would you have me be insensible to the tender protestations of this ardent passion which he shows for me?

Toi. Heaven forbid!

An. Just tell me; do not you see, with me, something from Heaven, some working of destiny, in the unexpected adventure of our acquaintance?

Toi. Yes.

An. Do not you find that this action of taking up my defence, without knowing me, is altogether that of a gentleman?

Toi. Yes.

An. That one could not have behaved more generously?

Toi. Agreed.

An. And that he did all this with the best possible grace?

Toi. Oh! yes.

An. Do not you think, Toinette, that he is well made in person?

Toi. Assuredly.

An. That he has the finest appearance in the world?

Toi. No doubt.

An. That his conversations, like his actions, have something noble?

Toi. That is certain.

An. That there could be nothing more passionate than what he says to me?

Toi. It is true.

An. And that there is nothing more annoying than the restraint under which I am kept, which stops all interchange of the sweet eagerness of this mutual affection with which Heaven inspires us?

Toi. You are right.

An. But, my dear Toinette, think you that he loves me as well as he says to me?

Toi. Eh! eh! these things are sometimes a little to be doubted. The vain pretences of love are very like the truth; and I have seen some great actors on that subject.

An. Ah! Toinette, what are you saying there? Alas! from the way he speaks, could it well be possible that he does not tell me the truth?

Toi. At any rate, you will be soon enlightened; and the resolve, of which he wrote to you yesterday, that he had taken to ask for your hand, is a prompt way to show you whether he loves you or not.[15] That will be the right proof.

AN. Ah! Toinette, if this one deceives me, I shall never in my life believe another man.

TOI. Here is your father coming back.

SCENE V.—ARGAN, ANGÉLIQUE, TOINETTE.

ARG. Daughter, I am going to tell you some news which, perhaps, you did not expect. You are being asked in marriage. What is this? You laugh? That is pleasant, yes, this word marriage! There is nothing more funny to young girls. Ah! nature, nature! From what I can perceive, daughter, I need hardly ask you, whether you would like to get married

AN. I must do all, father, that it pleases you to order me.

ARG. I am glad to have so obedient a daughter: so the matter is settled, and I have promised your hand.

AN. It is for me, father, blindly to follow all your wishes.

ARG. My wife, your step-mother, wished me to make you a nun, as well as your little sister Louison; and she has always persisted in it.

TOI. (Aside). The innocent has her reasons.

ARG. She would not consent to this marriage; but I have carried the day, and I have given my word.

AN. Ah! father, how obliged I am to you for all your goodness!

TOI. (To Argan). Truly, I like you for this; and this is the most sensible thing you ever did in all your life.

ARG. I have not yet seen the gentleman; but I have been told that I should be satisfied with him, and you also.

AN. Assuredly, father.

ARG. How! have you seen him?

AN. Since your consent authorizes me to open my heart to you, I will not dissemble, but tell you that accident

---

[15] Toinette prepares us for the mistake of the next scene, by informing us that Cléante had asked for the hand of Angélique. In the third act we shall see, however, that he had asked Béralde to do so.

made us acquainted six days ago, and that the request which has been made to you is the result of the inclination, which we, at this first sight, have conceived for each other.

ARG. They did not tell me this : but I am very glad of it, and it is much better that matters are so. They tell me that he is a tall young man, well made.

AN. Yes, father.

ARG. Of good stature.

AN. No doubt.

ARG. Agreeable in person.

AN. Assuredly.

ARG. Good-looking.

AN. Very much so.

ARG. Steady and well born.

AN. Quite.

ARG. Well bred.

AN. Could not possibly be better.

ARG. Who speaks Latin and Greek well.

AN. That is what I do not know.

ARG. And that he will take his diploma as a physician in three days.

AN. He, father?

ARG. Yes. Has he not told you?

AN. No indeed. Who told you?

ARG. Mr. Purgon.

AN. Does Mr. Purgon know him?

ARG. A pretty question ! He should know him, seeing that he is his nephew.

AN. Cléante, the nephew of Mr. Purgon ?

ARG. Which Cléante ? We are speaking of the one who has asked you in marriage.

AN. Well ! yes.

ARG. Well ! he is the nephew of Mr. Purgon, the son of his brother-in-law Dr. Diafoirus ; and this son's name is Thomas Diafoirus, and not Cléante ; and we have settled this match this morning, Mr. Purgon, Mr. Fleurant, and I ; and to-morrow this intended son-in-law is to be brought to me by his father. What is the matter ? You look altogether amazed !

AN. It is father, because I find that you have been speaking of one person, and that I understood another.

TOI. What! Sir, you could have formed that ridiculous design? And, with all the wealth you have, you would marry your daughter to a physician?

ARG. Yes. What are you interfering with, you slut, impudent hussy that you are?

TOI. Good gracious! gently. You begin immediately with invectives. Can we not argue together without getting into a passion? There, let us speak in cool blood. What is your reason, if you please, for such a match?

ARG. My reason is that, seeing myself infirm and ill as I am, I wish to have a son-in-law and relations who are physicians, so as to have the support of good assistance against my illness, to have in my own family the sources of the remedies which are necessary to me, and to be in a position of having consultations and prescriptions.

TOI. Well! that is giving your reason, and it is a pleasure to answer each other gently. But, Sir, consult your own conscience. Are you ill?

ARG. How! you wretch! am I ill! Am I ill, impudent hussey!

TOI. Well! yes, Sir; you are ill, let us not quarrel about that. Yes, you are very ill, I am agreed, and more ill than you imagine; that is settled. But your daughter must marry a husband for herself; and, not being ill, it is not necessary to give her a doctor.

ARG. It is for me that I give her this doctor; and a well disposed daughter ought to be delighted to marry that which is useful to the health of her father.

TOI. Upon my word, Sir, shall I as a friend give you an advice?

ARG. What is it, this advice?

TOI. Not to think of this marriage.

ARG. And the reason?

TOI. The reason is, that your daughter will not consent to it.

ARG. She will not consent to it?

TOI. No.

ARG. My daughter?

TOI. Your daughter. She will tell you that she has nothing to do with Mr. Diafoirus, nor with his son

Thomas Diafoirus, nor with any of the Diafoiruses in the world.

ARG. I have to do with them, besides that the match is more advantageous than the world imagines. Mr. Diafoirus has no other heir than this son ; and, what is more, Mr. Purgon, who has neither wife nor child, leaves him all his property in consideration of this marriage, and Mr. Purgon is a man who has eight thousand livres a-year.

TOI. He must have killed a good many people, to have made himself so rich !

ARG. Eight thousand livres a-year are something, without reckoning the father's property.

TOI. All that is well and good, Sir ; but I am always coming back to this : I advise you, between ourselves, to choose her another husband ; and she is not made to be Mrs. Diafoirus.

ARG. And I wish it to be so.

TOI. Eh, fie ! do not say so.

ARG. How ! do not say so.

TOI. Eh, no.

ARG. And why should I not say so ?

TOI. One would say you are not thinking of what you are saying.

ARG. One may say what one likes ; but I tell you that it is my wish that she shall fulfil my given promise.

TOI. No ; I am sure that she will not do so.

ARG. I will force her to do so.

TOI. She will not do so, I tell you.

ARG. She shall do so, or I shall put her in a convent.

TOI. You ?

ARG. I.

TOI. Good !

ARG. How ! good ?

TOI. You will not put her in a convent.

ARG. I will not put her in a convent ?

TOI. No.

ARG. No ?

TOI. No.

ARG Hoity toity ! This is pleasant ! I shall not put my daughter in a convent, if I wish it ?

TOI. No ; I tell you.

ARG. Who shall prevent me?

TOI. Yourself.

ARG. I!

TOI. Yes. You will not have the heart.

ARG. I shall have it.

TOI. You are jesting.

ARG. I am not jesting at all.

TOI. Your paternal tenderness will prevent you.

ARG. It will not prevent me.

TOI. A little tear or two, arms thrown round the neck, "My darling little papa," tenderly pronounced, will be enough to touch you.

ARG. All that will have no effect.

TOI. Yes, yes.

ARG. I tell you that I shall not go back from it.

TOI. Nonsense.

ARG. You must not say, Nonsense.

TOI. Good Heavens! I know you, you are naturally kind-hearted.

ARG. (*Getting angry*). I am not kind-hearted, and I am very spiteful when I wish to be so.[16]

TOI. Gently, Sir. You forget that you are ill.

ARG. I absolutely command her to prepare herself to take the husband I tell her.

TOI. And I absolutely forbid her to do anything of the kind.

ARG. Where in the world are we? and in what sort of audacity is this, for a slut of a servant to talk in this manner before her master?

TOI When a master forgets what he is doing, a sensible servant has a right to correct him.

ARG. (*Running after Toinette*). Ah! you insolent hussy, I shall have to knock you down.

TOI. (*Avoiding Argan, placing a chair between herself and him*). It is my duty to oppose myself to things which might disgrace you.

ARG. (*Running round the chair, with his stick, after Toinette*). Come here, come, that I may teach you how to speak.

---

16 This dialogue is copied almost literally from the Sixth Scene of the First Act of *The Rogueries of Scapin.*

TOI. (*Dodging away at the opposite side*).   I interest myself, as I ought to do, not to let you commit any folly.

ARG. (*Same business*).   You slut!

TOI. (*Same business*).   No, I shall never consent to this marriage.

ARG. (*Same business*).   You good-for-nothing.

TOI. (*Same business*).   I will not have her marry your Thomas Diafoirus.

ARG. (*Same business*).   Baggage!

TOI. (*Same business*).   She will obey me rather than you.

ARG. (*Stopping*).   Angélique, will you not stop this slut for me?

AN.   Eh! father, do not make yourself ill.

ARG. (*To Angelique*).   If you do not stop her for me, I will give you my curse.

TOI. (*Going*).   And I shall disinherit her, if she obeys you.

ARG. (*Throwing himself in his chair*).   Ah! Ah! I am exhausted.   This is enough to kill me.[17]

SCENE VI.—BÉLINE, ARGAN.

ARG   Ah! wife, come here.

BEL.   What ails you, my poor husband?

ARG.   Come here to my assistance.

BEL.   But what is the matter, dear?

ARG.   My darling!

BEL.   My pet!

ARG.   I have been put into a passion.

BEL.   Alas! poor dear husband! But how, my friend?

ARG.   Your slut of a Toinette has been more insolent than ever.

BEL.   Do not excite yourself.

ARG.   She has put me into a rage, my dear.

BEL.   Gently, my son.

ARG.   During an hour, she has opposed the things which I wish to do.

BEL.   There, there, gently.

---

[17] Compare the Second Scene of the Second Act of *Tartuffe*.   (See Vol. II.)

ARG. And she has had the effrontery to tell me that I am not ill.

BEL. She is an impertinent hussey.

ARG. You know, my heart, what is the case.

BEL. Yes, my heart, she is wrong.

ARG. My love, this wretch will kill me.

BEL. Eh! eh!

ARG. She is the cause of all my bile.

BEL. Do not get so angry.

ARG. And I have told you, I do not know how often, to get rid of her.

BEL. Good Heavens! child, there are neither men nor women servants who have not their faults. One is often obliged to put up with their bad qualities, for the sake of their good ones. This one is handy, careful, diligent, and above all faithful; and you know that we must be very cautious now-a-days with the folks we take.[18] Hullo! Toinette!

SCENE VII.—ARGAN, BÉLINE, TOINETTE.

TOI. Madam.

BEL. Why do you put my husband into a passion?

TOI. (*In a coaxing tone*). I, Madam? Alas! I do not know what you mean, and I strive to please master in everything.

ARG. Oh! the wretch!

TOI. He told us that he wished to give his daughter in marriage to the son of Mr. Diafoirus: I answered him that I thought that the match was advantageous to her, but that I believed he would do better to put her into a convent.

BEL. There is not much harm in that, and I think that she is right.

ARG. Ah! my love, do you believe her? She is a good-for-nothing; she has said a hundred insolent things to me.

BEL. Well! I believe you, my friend. There, calm yourself. Listen, Toinette: if ever you vex my husband,

---

[18] This defence of Toinette by Béline shows that she afterwards intends to use her; but we have already seen in the servant's exclamation " What an innocent woman!" that Toinette knows her well.

I will put you out of the house. There, now give me his furred cloak and some pillows, that I may make him comfortable in his chair. You are I do not know how. Pull your cap well over your ears : there is nothing that gives cold like catching a draught in the ears.

ARG. Ah ! my dear, how obliged I am for all the care you take of me.

BEL. (*Arranging the pillows which she puts round Argan*). Just lift yourself, that I may put this under you. Let us place this one to lean upon, and that one on the other side. Let us put this one behind your back, and the other one to support your head.

TOI. (*Rudely putting a pillow on his head*). And this one to keep the night dew away from you.

ARG. (*Rising and throwing his pillows at Toinette, who runs away*). Ah, you wretch ! you want to stifle me.

SCENE VIII.—ARGAN, BÉLINE.

BEL. Hullo ! hullo ! What is the matter now ?

ARG. (*Throwing himself into his chair*). Ah ! ah ! ah ! I am exhausted.

BEL. Why get into such a passion ? She thought of doing right.

ARG. My love, you do not know the spitefulness of the good-for-nothing. Ah ! she has entirely put me out ; and I shall want more than eight doses of medicine and twelve enemas to put all this right.

BEL. There, there, my little dear, try to quiet yourself a little.

ARG. My darling, you are my only consolation.

BEL. Poor dear child !

ARG. To try to acknowledge the love which you have for me, my heart, I wish, as I have told you, to make my will.

BEL. Ah, my friend. do not let us speak of this, I pray ; I cannot bear the thought ; and the very word, will, makes me shudder with pain.

ARG. I had told you to speak about it to your notary.

BEL. He is just inside. I brought him with me.

ARG. Make him come in, my love.

BEL. Alas! my friend, when one loves a husband well, one is hardly able to think of all this.

SCENE IX.—MR. DE BONNEFOI, BÉLINE, ARGAN.

ARG. Draw near, Mr. de Bonnefoi ; draw near. Take a seat, if you please. My wife has told me, Sir, that you are a very honest man, and altogether her friend ; and I have told her to speak to you about a will which I wish to make.

BEL. Alas ! I am not able to talk of these matters.

MR. DE B. She has explained your intentions to me, Sir, and what you purpose to do for her; and I must tell you on this score that you cannot give anything to your wife by your will.

ARG. But why?

MR. DE B. Common law is opposed to it. If you were in a country where there is statute law, it could be done ; but in Paris, and in all the countries where common law exists, at least in most of them, this cannot be ; and the disposition would be invalid. All the good which man and woman joined in wedlock can do to each other, is a mutual gift while living ; and then there must be no children, either of the two contracting parties, or of one of them, at the time of decease of the one who dies first.[19]

ARG. This is a very impertinent custom, that a husband can leave nothing to a wife by whom he is tenderly beloved, and who takes so much care of him ! I would feel inclined to consult my barrister, to see how I might act.

MR. DE B. It is not to barristers that you must go; for they are, as a rule, very strict on these matters, and imagine that it is a great crime to dispose of property contrary to law : they are people of difficulties, who are ignorant of the intricacies of one's conscience. There are other people to consult, who are very much more accommodating, who have expedients to glide gently over the law, and to make that right which is not allowed; who know how to smooth the difficulties of an affair, and to find means of eluding custom by some indirect advantage.

---

[19] This is according to articles 280 and 282 of the ancient Common Law of Paris.

Without this, where should we be every day? There must be some elasticity in affairs; otherwise we should do nothing, and I would not give a halfpenny for our profession.

Arg. My wife has indeed told me, Sir, that you are a very able and a very honest man. How am I to do, if you please, to give her my property, and to deprive my children of it?

Mr. de B. How are you to do? You can quietly choose an intimate friend of your wife's, to whom you will give, in due form, by your will, all that you can; and this friend shall afterwards give it all back to her. You can also contract a great many plausible obligations for the benefit of various creditors who will lend their names to your wife, and into whose hands they will put a declaration that what they did was only to benefit her. You can also, while you are alive, put into her hands ready money, or bills which you may make payable to the bearer.

Bel. Good Heavens! you must not torment yourself about all that. If you should happen to die, I should no longer remain in this world.

Arg. My darling!

Bel. Yes, my friend, if I am unfortunate enough to lose you . . .

Arg. My dear wife!

Bel. Life will no longer be anything to me.

Arg. My love!

Bel. And I shall follow you, to show the tenderness I have for you.

Arg. My darling, you rend my heart! Console yourself, I pray you.

Mr. de B. (*To Béline*). These tears are unseasonable. Matters have not come to that yet.

Bel. Ah! Sir, you do not know what a husband is whom one loves tenderly.

Arg. All the regret which I shall have, if I die, my dear, is not to have a child by you. Mr. Purgon had told me that I should have one.

Mr. de B. This may come yet.

Arg. I must make my will, love, in the manner this gentleman says; but as a precaution, I will put into your hands the twenty thousand francs in gold which I have in the wainscoting of the recess of my bed, and two bills payable to the bearer, one from Mr. Damon, and the other from Mr. Gérante.

BEL. No, no, I will have nothing of all this. By the bye ! . . . how much say you is there in your recess ?

ARG. Two thousand francs, my love.

BEL. Do not speak to me of property, I pray you. By the bye ! . . . for how much are the two bills.

ARG. They are, my dear, one for four thousand francs, and the other for six.

BEL. All the riches in the world, my friend, are nothing compared with you.

MR. DE B. (*To Argan*). Shall we proceed to the making of the will ?

ARG. Yes, Sir ; but we shall be more at ease in my little study. Pray, my love, conduct me.

BEL. Come, my poor dear child.

SCENE X.—ANGÉLIQUE, TOINETTE.

TOI. They are with a notary and I heard them speaking about a will. Your step-mother does not go to sleep ; and it is no doubt some conspiracy against your interests to which she drives your father.

AN. Let him dispose of his property according as he likes, provided he does not dispose of my heart. You see, Toinette, the violent designs which they have upon it. Do not abandon me, I pray you, in the strait I am in.

TOI. I, abandon you ! I would rather die. Your step-mother may make me her confidante, and draw me in to her interests as much as she likes, I was never able to like her ; and have always been on your side. Let me manage ; I shall do everything to serve you ; but, to do so with more effect, I shall change my tactics, conceal the interest I take in you, and pretend to enter into the feelings of your father and step-mother.

AN. Try, I beseech you to send Cléante word of the marriage that has been resolved upon.

TOI. I have no one that I can employ for this errand but the old usurer, Punch, my lover ; and it will cost me

some sweet words, which I do not begrudge for your sake.[20]
To-day it is too late, but the first thing to-morrow I shall
send for him, and he will be delighted to . . .

SCENE XI.—BÉLINE *in the house*, ANGÉLIQUE, TOINETTE.

BEL. Toinette!

TOI. (*To Angélique*). I am being called. Good-night.
Rely upon me.

FIRST INTERLUDE.

The Scene changes and represent a town.

*Punch, in the night, comes to serenade his mistress. He
is first of all interrupted by the violins, with which he gets
into a passion, and afterwards by the watch, composed of
dancers and musicians.*

PUNCH. (*Alone*). O, love, love, love, love! Poor
Punch, what a deuce of a fancy has got into your brain!
What are you amusing yourself with, wretched idiot that
you are? You leave the care of your business, and let
your affairs go anyhow; you no longer eat, you do hardly drink, you lose your rest at night; and all this, for
whom? For a dragon, a downright dragon; a she-devil
who repulses you, and mocks at all you say to her. But
it is no good arguing on that point. You will it so,
Cupid: one must be a fool, like many others. It is not
the wisest thing for a man of my age; but what can
I do to it? One cannot be wise when one will, and old
brains get out of order as well as young ones. I have
come to see if I cannot soften my tigress by a serenade.
At times there is nothing so touching as a lover who
comes to sing his plaints to the bolts and bars of his mistress's door. (*After having taken his lute*). Here is something to accompany my voice with. Oh night! O dear
night! carry my love-sick plaints to the bed of my ob-
durate one.

---

[20] Toinette mentions Punch only to introduce the following Interlude.

Night and day I love and adore you.
I seek a yes that shall restore me;
But if you answer, No,
Fair ingrate, I shall die.

Hope deferred
Makes the heart sick;
And far from you
It consumes its hours.
This sweet error
That does persuade me
That my grief is about to end,
Alas! lasts too long.
Thus, through loving you too much, I languish
and I die.

Night and day I love and adore you.
I seek a yes that shall restore me;
But if you answer, No,
Fair ingrate, I shall die.

If you are not asleep,
Think at least
Of the wounds
You give to my heart.
Ah! pretend at least,
For my consolation,
If you will kill me,
To be in the wrong;
Your pity will assuage my martyrdom.

Night and day I love and adore you.
I seek a yes that shall restore me;
But if you answer, No,
Fair ingrate, I shall die [21]

---

[21] The original is in Italian.

SCENE II.—PUNCH, AN OLD WOMAN, SHOWING HERSELF
AT THE WINDOW, AND ANSWERING PUNCH, MOCKING HIM.

OLD WOMAN. (*Sings.*)—

Gallants, who, at every moment, with deceitful looks,
      And lying wishes,
      And false sighs,
      And perfidious tor es,
      Pride yourself on being faithful,
      Ah! do not deceive yourselves.
      From experience I know
      That neither constancy nor faithfulness
      Is to be found in you.
Ah! how foolish is she who believes you!

      These languishing regards
      Do not inspire me with any love,
      These ardent sighs
      Do not inflame me,
      I swear to you on my faith.
      Unhappy gallant!
      My heart, insensible to your complaint,
      Will ever laugh at it:
      Believe me;
      For from experience I know
    That neither constancy nor faithfulness
    Is to be found in you.
Ah! how foolish is she who believes you![22]

SCENE III.—PUNCH, VIOLINS BEHIND THE SCENES.

The violins commence an air.

PUNCH. What impertinent harmony comes to interrupt
my song!

The violins continue to play.

PUNCH. Peace; there! be still, you violins.   Let me
bewail at my ease the cruelties of my inexorable fair one.

The violins continue.

PUNCH. Keep still, I tell you: it is I who wish to sing.

---

[22] The original is also in Italian.

The violins continue.

PUNCH. Silence then!

The violins continue.

PUNCH. Good gracious!

The violins continue.

PUNCH. Ah!

The violins continue.

PUNCH. Is this in fun?

The violins continue.

PUNCH. Ah! what a noise!

The violins continue.

PUNCH. May the devil take you!

The violins continue.

PUNCH. I am bursting with rage!

The violins continue.

PUNCH. You will not be still then! Ah! Heaven be praised!

The violins continue.

PUNCH. What! again?

The violins continue.

PUNCH. A plague upon these violins!

The violins continue.

PUNCH. What silly music this!

The violins continue.

PUNCH. (*Singing, in imitation of the violins*). La, la, la, la, la, la.

The violins continue.

PUNCH. (*Same*). La, la, la, la, la, la.

The violins continue.

PUNCH. (*Same*). La, la, la, la, la, la.

The violins continue.

PUNCH. (*Same*). La, la, la, la, la, la.

The violins continue.

PUNCH. (*Same*). La, la, la, la, la, la.

The violins continue.

PUNCH. Upon my word this amuses me. Go on, gentlemen violin-players ; you are giving me great pleasure. (*No longer hearing anything*). But continue, I pray you.

Scene IV. Punch, alone.

This is the way to quiet them. Music is accustomed not to do what we wish. And now, it is my turn. I must prelude a bit, and play a little piece before singing, so as the better to catch my tone. (*He takes his lute, upon which he pretends to play, imitating with his lips and tongue the sound of that instrument*). Plan, plan. plan, plin, plin, plin. This is a nasty time to tune a lute to. Plin, plin, plin. Plin, tan, plan. Plin, plan. The strings do not hold in such weather. Plin, plin. I hear some noise. Let us put our lute against the door.

Scene V.—Punch ; Archers passing in the street, attracted by the noise which they hear.

ARCH. (*Singing*). Who goes there ! who goes there ?

PUNCH. (*Softly*). What the devil is that ? Is it the fashion to speak in music ?

ARCH. Who goes there ? who goes there ? who goes there ?

PUNCH. (*Frightened*). I, I, I.

ARCH. Who goes there ? who goes there ? I ask you.

PUNCH. I, I, I tell you.

ARCH. And who are you ? who are you ?

PUNCH. I, I, I, I, I, I.

ARCH. Tell your name, tell your name, without delaying longer.

PUNCH. (*Pretending to be courageous*). My name is, Go and get yourself hanged.

ARCH. Here, comrades, here.

And seize the insolent who answers us thus.

First Entry of the Ballet.

The whole of the watch come, seeking for Punch in the dark.

Violins and Dancers.

PUNCH. Who goes there?

Violins and Dancers.

PUNCH. Who are the scoundrels whom I hear?

Violins and Dancers.

PUNCH. Ugh!

Violins and Dancers.

PUNCH. Hullo! my servants! my lacqueys!

Violins and Dancers.

PUNCH. S'death!

Violins and Dancers.

PUNCH. S'blood!

Violins and Dancers.

PUNCH. I shall knock some of them down.

Violins and Dancers.

PUNCH. Here! Champagne, Poitevin, Picard, Basque, Breton.[23]

Violins and Dancers.

PUNCH. Just hand me my musket. . . .

Violins and Dancers.

PUNCH. (*Pretending to discharge a Pistol*). Paff.
    (*They all fall down, and run away afterwards*).

SCENE VI.—PUNCH (*Alone*).

Ah! ah! ah! ah! what a fright I have given them! They must be silly people to be afraid of me, who am afraid of others. Upon my word, there is nothing like being artful in this world. If I had not imitated the

---

[23] See *Pretentious Young Ladies*, Vol. I., page 162, note 40.

grand nobleman, and pretended to be brave, they would not have failed to lock me up.   Ah! ah! ah! (*The Archers draw near, and having heard what he said, catch him by the collar*).

SCENE VII. – PUNCH; ARCHERS, *singing.*

ARCH. (*Seizing Punch*).
We have got him.   Here, comrades, here!
Make haste; bring a light.
(*The whole of the watch come with lanterns*).

SCENE VIII.—PUNCH; ARCHERS, *dancing and singing.*

ARCH. Ah! traitor; ah! rogue, it is you?
Wretch, cur, hangdog, impudent, audacious,
Insolent, brazen-faced fellow, scoundrel, cut-
purse thief,
You dare give us a fright!
PUNCH. Gentlemen, it is because I was drunk.
ARCH. No, no, no; no arguing:
We must teach you to behave.
To prison, quick, to prison.
PUNCH. Gentlemen, I am not a thief.
ARCH. To prison.
PUNCH. I am a citizen of the town.
ARCH. To prison.
PUNCH. What have I done?
ARCH. To prison, quick, to prison.
PUNCH. Let me go, gentlemen.
ARCH. No.
PUNCH. I beseech you!
ARCH. No.
PUNCH. Eh!
ARCH. No.
PUNCH. I beseech you.
ARCH. No, no.
PUNCH. Gentlemen.
ARCH. No, no, no.
PUNCH. If you please!
ARCH. No, no.
PUNCH. For charity!
ARCH. No, no.

PUNCH. In Heaven's name!

ARCH. No, no.

PUNCH. Have mercy.

ARCH. No, no, no arguing,
   We must teach you to behave.
   To prison, quick, to prison.

PUNCH. Eh! gentlemen, is there nothing capable of softening your hearts?

ARCH. It is easy to move us;
   And we are more tender-hearted than you
     would believe.
   Only give us six pistoles to drink your health
     with,
   And we will let you go.

PUNCH. Alas! gentlemen, I assure you that I have not a penny upon me.

ARCH. In default of six pistoles,
   Choose then without ado
   To receive thirty fillips,
   Or twelve blows with the stick.

PUNCH. If it must be, and that I must pass through that, I choose the fillips.

ARCH. Come then, prepare yourself,
   And count the fillips well.

Second Entry of the Ballet.

The dancing archers give him the fillips, keeping time with the music.

PUNCH. (*Counting the fillips which they are giving him*). One and two, three and four, five and six, seven and eight, nine and ten, eleven and twelve, and thirteen, and fourteen, and fifteen.

ARCH. Ah! ah! you will pass through it!
   Let us begin once more.

PUNCH. Ah! gentlemen, my poor head can stand this no longer, and you have just made it like a cooked apple. I prefer the blows with the stick to your beginning again.

ARCH. Be it so. Since the stick has more charms
     for you,
   You shall be satisfied.

Third Entry of the Ballet.

The dancing archers give him blows with the stick, keeping time to the music.

PUNCH. (*Counting the blows of the stick*). One, two, three, four, five, six. Ah! ah! ah! I can resist no longer. Here, gentlemen, here are six pistoles which I give you.

ARCH. Ah! what a gentleman! Ah! what a great and generous soul;
Good-bye, Sir; good-bye, Mr. Punch.

PUNCH. Gentlemen, I wish you good-night.

ARCH. Good-bye, Sir; good-bye, Mr. Punch.

PUNCH. Your servant.

ARCH. Good-bye, Sir; good-bye, Mr. Punch.

PUNCH. Your very humble servant.

ARCH. Good-bye, Sir; good-bye, Mr. Punch.

PUNCH. Until we meet again.

Fourth Entry of the Ballet.

They all dance from joy, at the money they have received.

ACT II.

The scene represents Argan's room.

SCENE I.—CLÉANTE, TOINETTE.

TOI. (*Not recognizing Cléante*). What is your pleasure, Sir?

CLE. What is your pleasure?

TOI. Ah! ah! it is you! What surprise! What come you to do here?

CLE. To learn my fate, to speak to the amiable Angélique, to consult the sentiments of her heart, and to ask her decision about this fatal match of which I have been informed.

TOI. Yes; but you cannot speak so inconsiderately to Angélique: it requires secrecy, and you have been told of the careful watch that is kept over her, that she is never allowed to go out, nor to speak to any one; and that it was only the curiosity of an old aunt, who obtained permission for us to go to this comedy, which gave rise to your passion; and we have taken good care not to speak of this adventure.

CLE. For this reason do I not come as Cléante, and in the guise of her lover; but as a friend of her music-teacher, of whom I have obtained leave to say that he sends me in his stead.

TOI. Here comes her father. Just retire a little, and let me tell him that you are there.

SCENE II.—ARGAN, TOINETTE.

ARG. (*Believing himself alone, and not noticing Toinette*). Mr. Purgon has told me to walk about this morning, in my room, a dozen times up and a dozen times down, but I have forgotten to ask him whether it should be the length or the breadth of the room.

TOI. Sir, here is a . . .

ARG. Speak low, you hang-dog. You shake my brain, and you forget that invalids should not be spoken to so loudly.

TOI. I wished to say to you, Sir . . .

ARG. Speak low, I tell you.

TOI. Sir . . .   (*She pretends to speak.*

ARG. Eh?

TOI. I was telling you that . . .

              (*She again pretends to speak.*

ARG. What do you say?

TOI. (*Loud*). I say that there is a man who wishes to speak to you.

ARG. Let him come here. (*Toinette beckons Cléante to draw near*).

SCENE III.—ARGAN, CLÉANTE, TOINETTE.

CLE. Sir . . .

TOI. (*To Cléante*). Do not speak so loud, for fear of shaking master's brain.

CLE. Sir, I am charmed to find you up, and to see that you are convalescent.

TOI. (*Pretending to be angry*). How! convalescent! That is false. Master is always ill.

CLE. I heard it said that Mr. Argan was getting better; and I find that he looks well.

TOI. What do you mean by "he looks well?" Master looks very bad; and they are impertinent fellows who have told you that he was better. He has never been worse.

ARG. She is right.

TOI. He walks, sleeps, eats and drinks like other people; but that does not prevent him from being very ill.

ARG. That is true.

CLE. I am sorely grieved, Sir. I come from your daughter's singing-master; he has been obliged to go into the country for a few days, and, as his intimate friend, he sends me in his stead to continue the lessons, for fear that, in interrupting them, she should forget what she already knows.

ARG. Very good. (*To Toinette*). Call Angélique.

TOI. I think, Sir, that it would be better to take this gentleman to her room.

ARG. No. Fetch her here.

TOI. He could not give her a proper lesson, if they be not alone.

ARG. Yes, yes.

TOI. It will upset you, Sir; and there should be nothing to excite you, and to shake your brain, in the state you are in.

ARG. Not at all, not at all: I love music, and I shall be glad to . . . Ah! here she is. (*To Toinette*). Go you and see, you, whether my wife is dressed.

SCENE IV.—ARGAN, ANGÉLIQUE, CLÉANTE.

ARG. Come here, daughter. Your music-master is gone to the country; and here is some one whom he sends in his stead to teach you.

AN. (*Recognizing Cléante*). Oh Heavens!

ARG. What is the matter? Whence this surprise?

AN. It is . . .

ARG. What? What moves you in this manner?

AN. It is a most surprising adventure that is happening here, father.

ARG. How?

AN. I dreamt last night that I was in the greatest difficulty, and that some one, just like this gentleman, presented himself to me, of whom I implored assistance, and who came to deliver me from the trouble in which I was; and my surprise was great to see unexpectedly, on arriving here, what was in my mind all night.

CLE. It is being very fortunate to occupy your thoughts, whether sleeping or waking; and my happiness would be great, no doubt, if you were in some danger, from which you deemed me worthy to extricate you. There is nothing I would not do to . . .

SCENE V.—ARGAN, ANGÉLIQUE, CLÉANTE, TOINETTE.

TOI. (*To Argan*). Upon my word, Sir, I am entirely on your side this time, and I retract everything which I said yesterday. Here are Mr. Diafoirus, the father, and Mr. Diafoirus, his son, who come to pay you a visit. What a nice son-in-law you will have! You shall see the handsomest young fellow possible, and the wittiest. He has said but two words which have delighted me, and your daughter will be charmed with him.

ARG. (*To Cléante, who pretends to go*). Do not go, Sir. My daughter is about to be married, and her intended, whom she has not seen as yet, has just come.

CLE. It is doing me a great honour, Sir, to wish me to assist at so pleasant an interview.

ARG. He is the son of a very able physician; and the marriage is to take place in four days.

CLE. Very good.

ARG. Just mention it to her music-master, so that he may be at the wedding.

CLE. I will not fail to do so.

ARG. I invite you also.

CLE. You are doing me much honour.

TOI. Come, let us place ourselves in position; here they are.

SCENE VI.—MR. DIAFOIRUS, THOMAS DIAFOIRUS, ARGAN, ANGÉLIQUE, CLÉANTE, TOINETTE, A LACQUEY.

ARG. (*Putting his hand to his cap, without taking it off*). Mr. Purgon, Sir, has forbidden me to uncover my head. You belong to the profession: you know the consequences.

Mr. D. In all our visits we aim at bringing help to those who are ill, and not inconvenience

(*Argan and Mr. Diafoirus speak at the same time.*).

ARG. I receive, Sir,

MR. D. We come here, Sir,

ARG. With great joy,

MR. D. My son Thomas, and I,

ARG. The honour which you do me,

MR. D. To assure you, Sir,

ARG. And I should have wished . . .

MR. D. How delighted we are . . .

ARG. To be able to go to you . . .

MR. D. At the graciousness you show us . . .

ARG. To assure you of it;

MR. D. In receiving us . . .

ARG. But you know, Sir,

MR. D. To the honour, Sir,

ARG. What it is to be a poor invalid,

MR. D. Of your alliance;

ARG. Who can do nothing else . . .

MR. D. And to assure you . .

ARG. Than to tell you in this spot . . .

Mr. D. That in all things pertaining to our profession,

ARG. That, he will seek every opportunity . . .

MR. D. As well as in everything else,

ARG. To tell you, Sir,

MR. D. We shall always be prepared, Sir.

ARG. That he is entirely at your service.

MR. D. To prove our zeal to you. (*To his son*). Come Thomas, approach and pay your respects.

THOM. (*To Mr. Diafoirus*). Is it not with the father that I ought to begin? [24]

Mr. D. Yes.

THOM. (*To Argan*). Sir, I come to salute, to acknowledge, to cherish, and to revere in you a second father, but a second father to whom, I make bold to say, I find myself more indebted than to the first. The first engendered me; but

---

[24] In the edition of Molière's works of 1682 is the following note: " Mr. Thomas Diafoirus is a great booby. having newly left the schools, and doing everything awkwardly and at the wrong time."

you have chosen me; he received me through necessity,
but you have accepted me out of kindness.[25]   What I have
from him is the work of his body; but what I have from
you is the work of your will; and inasmuch as the spirit-
ual faculties are above the corporal, so much the more do
I owe you, and so much the more do I hold precious this future filiation, of which I come this day to render to you,
before-hand, the very humble and very respectful homage.

Toi. Long life to the colleges which turn out so able a
man!

Thom. (*To Mr. Diafoirus*). Has this been right, father?

Mr. D. Optime.

Arg. (*To Angélique*).   Come, salute this gentleman.

Thom. (*To Mr. Diafoirus*).   Shall I kiss her?[26]

Mr. D. Yes, yes.

Thom. (*To Angélique*).   Madam, it is with justice,
that Heaven has conceded you the title of stepmother,
since we . . .

Arg. (*To Thomas Diafoirus*).   This is not my wife, it is
my daughter to whom you are speaking.

Thom. Where is she then?

Arg. She will be here directly.

Thom. Shall I wait, father, until she comes?

Mr. D. Offer your compliments to the young lady.

Thom. Miss, neither more nor less than the statue of
Memnon gave forth an harmonious sound, when it was
illuminated by the rays of the sun, so do I feel myself
animated by a sweet transport of the appearance of the
sun of your charms;[27] and as naturalists observe that the
flower named heliotrope turns incessantly towards that
star of the day, so shall my heart henceforth turn towards
the resplendent star of your adorable eyes, as to its only
pole.   Permit me then, Miss, to bring to-day to the altar
of your charms the offer of that heart which aspires and

---

[25] This beginning seems imitated from a passage of a speech of Cicero
—*Ad Quirites, post reditum.*

[26] In the Elzevir edition of this play we find here: "He first makes a
bow, and then turns his face towards his father. Isabelle (Angélique)
receives the kiss with great disdain, while turning her head towards Cato
(Toinette)."

[27] The Abbé d'Aubignac, in a dissertation against Corneille, uses nearly
the same simile.

aims at no other glory than to be, all its life, Miss, your very humble, very obedient, and very faithful servant and husband.

TOI. See what it is to study! one learns to say beautiful things.

ARG. (*To Cléante*). Eh! What say you to this?

CLE. That this gentleman does wonders, and that, if he be as good a physician as he is an orator, it would be a pleasure to be counted among his patients.

TOI. Assuredly. It will be something admirable, if his cures are as good as the speeches which he makes.

ARG. Come, quick, my chair, and seats for everybody. (*Servants hand chairs*). Place yourself there, daughter. (*To Mr. Diafoirus*). You see, Sir, that everyone admires your son; and I think you very fortunate in finding yourself possessed of such a boy.

MR. D. Sir, it is not because I am his father; but I can say that I have reason to be satisfied with him, and that all who see him speak of him as a youth who has no harm in him. He never had a very lively imagination, nor that brilliant wit which is noticed in some; but it is exactly on this account that I have argued well of his judgment, a quality requisite for the exercise of our art. He never was, when little, what they call sharp and wide-awake; he was always seen to be gentle, peaceable and taciturn, never saying a word and never playing at those little games which are called infantine. They had all the difficulty in the world in teaching him to read, and at nine years of age, he did not yet know his letters. Good, said I to myself, the backward trees are those that bear the best fruit. One cuts into marble with far more difficulty than into sand; but things are preserved much longer there; and that slowness of apprehension, that dulness of imagination, is the sign of a future good judgment. When I sent him to college, he found it very hard, but he bore up against the difficulties; and his tutors always praised him to me for his assiduity and his application. In short, by dint of hammering, he has gloriously obtained his diplomas; and I may say, without vanity, that in the two years after he took his degree, there is no candidate who has made more noise than he in all the disputes of our school.

He has rendered himself formidable; and there is no act propounded upon which he does not argue as long as he can for the contrary proposition. He is firm in a dispute, strenuous as a Turk in his principles, and pursues an argument into the farthest recesses of logic. But, that which above all pleases me in him, and in which he follows my example, is that he attaches himself blindly to the opinions of the ancients, and that he never would understand or listen to the reasonings and experiments of the pretended discoveries of our age in reference to the circulation of the blood, and other opinions of the same kind.[28]

THOM. (*Drawing from his pocket a large thesis rolled up, which he presents to Angélique*). I have defended a thesis against the circulators, which, with the permission of your father (*Bowing to Argan*), I make bold to offer to this young lady, as a homage which I owe to her of the first fruits of my mind.

AN. It is a useless piece of furniture to me, Sir, and I am no judge in these matters.

TOI. (*Taking the thesis*). Give it all the same; it is worth taking for the picture; it will do to decorate our room.

THOM. (*Again bowing to Argan*). Once more, with the permission of your father, I invite you to come and see, one of these days, for your amusement, the dissection of a woman, upon which I am to lecture.

TOI. The entertainment will be pleasant. There are some people who treat their mistresses to a comedy; but to provide a dissection is more gallant.

MR. D. For the rest, as regards the requisite qualities for wedlock and propagation, I assure you that, according to the rules of our physicians, he is such as could be wished for; that he possesses in a praiseworthy degree the prolific virtue, and that he is of the proper temperament to engender and procreate well-conditioned children.

ARG. Is it not your intention, Sir, to push him at

---

[28] Harvey discovered the circulation of the blood in 1619, and many discussions took place in France on that subject, which were not completely ended when Molière's last play was performed. This same year (1673) Louis XIV. instituted at the *Jardin des Plantes* a special chair for anatomy.

Court, and to procure for him the place of a physician in
ordinary?

MR. D. To speak frankly to you, our profession when
near the great has never appeared pleasant to me; and I
have always found that it does better for us to remain with
the public. The public is easy to deal with; you are re-
sponsible for your actions to no one; and provided you
follow the current of the rules of your art, you need not be
uneasy about what may happen. But what is vexatious
with the great, is that, when they fall ill, they absolutely
wish their physicians to cure them.

TOI. That is funny! and they are very impertinent to
wish you gentlemen to cure them! You are not near them
for that; you are there only to receive your fees, and to
order them remedies; it is for them to get better, if they
can.

MR. D. That is true; one is only obliged to treat people according to the rules.

ARG. (*To Cléante*). Just make my daughter sing a little
before the company, Sir.

CLÉ. I was awaiting your orders, Sir; and an idea has
just struck me, to entertain the company, to sing with the
lady a scene from an operetta which has lately been composed. (*To Angélique, giving her a paper*). There, this is
your part.

AN. I?

CLÉ. (*Softly to Angélique*). Do not make any objection
to it, pray, and let me make you understand what the scene
is which we are to sing. (*Aloud*). I have no voice for
singing; but in this case it is sufficient that I can make
myself heard; and you will have the kindness to excuse
me, by the necessity under which I find myself to make
the young lady sing.[29]

ARG. Is the poetry good?

CLÉ. It is properly called a little improvised opera; and
you will only hear sung rhythmical prose, or some sort of
blank verse, such as affection and necessity might suggest

---

[29] A similar scene is also to be found in *The Blunderer* (see Vol. I.), *The
School for Husbands* (see Vol. I.), *Love is the Physician* (see Vol. II.),
The Sicilian (see Vol. II.), and *The Miser* (see Vol. III.)

to two persons, who say those things out of their own
heads, and speak on the spur of the moment.

ARG. Very good. Let us listen.

CLE. This is the plot of the scene : A shepherd was
attentively watching the beauties of a spectacle which had
just commenced, when his attention was disturbed by a
noise which he heard at his side. He turns round, and
sees a coarse fellow, who with insolent words insults a
shepherdess. Immediately he espouses the interests of
that sex to which all men owe homage ; and after having
given the coarse fellow the punishment due to his insolence, he comes back to the shepherdess, and beholds a
young person, who, from the most lovely eyes which he
had ever seen, drops tears which he thinks the most beautiful in the world. Alas ! says he to himself, can people
be capable of insulting so amiable a being ! and what in-
human monster, what barbarian would not be touched by
such tears ? He busies himself to stop them, these tears
which he thinks so beautiful ; and the gentle shepherdess
takes care at the same time to thank him for his slight
service, but in a manner so charming, so tender and so
impassioned, that the shepherd cannot resist it ; and every
glance, is a dart full of fire with which his heart feels itself
pierced. Is there ought, said he, that could deserve the
sweet words of such an acknowledgment ? And what
would we not do, to what services, to what dangers would
we not feel delighted to run, to attract to ourselves, but
for one moment, the moving tenderness of so grateful a
heart ! The whole of the spectacle is enacted without his
paying the least attention to it ; but he complains that it
is too short, for the end will separate him from his adorable shepherdess ; and from this first sight, from this first
moment, he brings back with him all that can be most
intense in a passion of several years' duration. Behold
him immediately experiencing all the ills of absence, and
he is tortured by seeing no longer her whom he has seen
such a short time. He does all he can to enjoy this sight
once more, of which he preserves night and day so precious a recollection ; but the great restraint under which
his shepherdess is kept deprives him of every opportunity.
The violence of his passion makes him resolve to ask for

the hand of the adorable fair one, without whom he can
no longer live ; and he obtains her permission by means
of a note which he has the skill to have conveyed to her.
But, at the same time, he is informed that the father of
his fair one has projected a marriage with some one else,
and that everything is being prepared to celebrate the
ceremony.[30] Judge how cruel is the blow to the heart of
this sad shepherd ! Behold him overwhelmed by a mortal
grief; he cannot bear the horrible thought of seeing all
he loves in the arms of another ; and in despair, his love
makes him find the means of introducing himself into the
house of his shepherdess to learn her feelings, and to know
from her the fate to which he is to submit.   He there
meets with the preparations for all that he fears ; he wit-
nesses the coming of the unworthy rival whom the whims
of a father oppose to the tenderness of his love ; he sees
him triumphant, this ridiculous rival, near the gentle
shepherdess, as if the conquest were sure ; and this sight
fills him with anger which he can scarcely master ; he
darts painful glances at her whom he adores ; and the
respect for her, and the presence of her father, prevent
his saying anything to her except by his looks ; but at
last he breaks through all restraint, and the transport of
his passion obliges him thus to speak—(*He sings*)

> Beauteous Philis, it is too much, it is too
>   much to suffer ;
> Let us break this cruel silence, and bare your
>   thoughts to me.
> Tell me my fate.
> Am I to live? am I to die?
> AN. (*Singing*). You behold me, Tircis, sad and melan-
>   choly,
> At the preparations for the marriage which alarms
>   you.
> To Heaven I lift my eyes, I look at you, I sigh ;
> Need I to tell you more?

---

[30] Molière has borrowed this tale of Cléante most probably from the
Sanish of Francisco de Roxas, which had already been used by Thomas
Corneille, in *Don Bertrand de Cigarral*, a comedy, performed in 1650.

Arg. Lack-a-day! I did not think that my daughter
was so clever as to sing thus at first sight, without hesi-
tating.

Cle. Alas! fair Philis,
        Can it be that the enamoured Tircis
        Could be happy enough
        To find a place in your heart?

An. I do not refuse to acknowledge it, in this exceed-
            ing grief;
        Yes, Tircis, I love you.

Cle. O word full of charms!
        Have I heard rightly? Alas!
        Say it once more, Philis, so that I may not doubt.

An. Yes, Tircis, I love you.

Cle. For mercy's sake, once more, Philis.

An. I love you.

Cle. Repeat it a hundred times; do not get weary.

An. I love you, I love you;
        Yes, Tircis, I love you.

Cle. Ye gods, ye kings, who look down upon the world
            beneath your feet,
        Can you compare your happiness with mine?
        But, Philis, one thought
        Comes to trouble this sweet bliss.
        A rival, a rival . . .

An. Ah! I hate him more than death;
        And his presence is to me, as it is to you,
        A cruel torture.

Cle. But a father wishes to compel you to obey his
wishes.

An. Sooner, sooner will I die
        Than ever consent to it;
        Sooner, sooner will I die, sooner will I die.[31]

Arg. And what says the father to all this?

Cle. He says nothing.

Arg. That is an idiot of a father, to suffer all this nonsense without saying anything.

_____

[31] La Grange and the wife of Molière had a great success in this scene,
as it is said in the Sixth of the *Entretiens Galants*, *about Music*, published
in Paris in 1681.

CLE. (*Wishing to continue to sing*).

Ah! my love . . .

· ARG. No, no; this is enough of it. This comedy sets a very bad example. The shepherd Tircis is an impertinent fellow, and the shepherdess Philis is an impudent hussy to speak in that way before her father. (*To Angélique*). Show me this paper. Ah! ah! but where are the words which you have spoken? There is nothing but music written there?

CLE. Do not you know, Sir, that it has been recently invented to write the words with the notes in one? [32],

ARG. Very good. I am your servant, Sir; good-bye. We could have very well dispensed with your impertinent opera.

CLE. I thought to amuse you.

ARG. Nonsense does not amuse. Ah! here comes my wife.

SCENE VII.—BÉLINE, ARGAN, ANGÉLIQUE, MR. DIAFOIRUS, THOMAS DIAFOIRUS, TOINETTE.

ARG. My love, this is the son of Mr. Diafoirus.

THOM. Madam, it is with justice that Heaven has granted you the title of stepmother, for we see in your face . . . [33]

BEL. Sir, I am delighted to have come here opportunely, to enjoy the honour of seeing you.

THOM. For we see in your face . . . for we see in your face . . . Madam, you have interrupted me in the midst of my period, and that has confused my memory.

MR. D. Thomas, reserve this for another opportunity.

ARG. My pet, I would have wished you to be here just now.

TOI. Ah! Madam, you have lost a great deal in not having been here at the second father, at the statue of Memnon, and at the flower called heliotrope.

ARG. Come, daughter, put your hand in this gentleman's, and pledge him your faith, as to your husband.

---

[32] In the Elzevir edition of the play, Cléante pretends that the words of the duet are old and well known.

[33] Thomas Diafoirus utters a compliment which he has studied, but cannot finish it. *Belle-mère* means stepmother, but *belle mère* handsome mother.

AN. Father . . .

ARG. Well! father! What does this mean.

AN. Pray, do not hurry matters. Give us at least time to know each other, and to see grow up in us that inclination for one another which is so necessary to form a perfect union.

THOM. As for me, Miss, it is already entirely grown up in me; and I have no need to wait any longer.

AN. If you are so prompt, Sir, it is not the same with me; and I confess to you that your merit has not as yet made any impression on my heart.

ARG. Oh! well, well; there will be ample leisure for that when you are married.

AN. Ah! father, give me some time, I pray you. Wedlock is a chain to which we should never subject a heart by force; and if this gentleman is a man of honour, he ought not to wish to accept a person who would be his by coercion.

THOM. *Nego consequentiam*, Miss; and I may be a man of honour, and still wish to accept you from the hands of your father.

AN. It is a bad means of making yourself beloved by any one by doing her violence.

THOM. We read of the ancients, Miss, that their custom was to carry away by force, from the homes of their fathers, the daughters who were led to marriage, so that it might not appear to be by their own consent that they flew into the arms of a man.

AN. The ancients, Sir, are the ancients; and we are the people of the present day. Pretences are not at all necessary in our age; and when a marriage pleases us, we know well enough how to go to it, without being dragged to it. Have patience; if you love me, Sir, you ought to wish everything that I wish.

THOM. Yes, Miss, up to the interests of my love, exclusively.

AN. But the great sign of love is to submit to the wishes of her whom we love.

THOM. *Distinguo*, Miss. In what concerns not her possession, *concedo;* but in what concerns it, *nego*.

TOI. You may argue as much as you please. The

gentleman is fresh from college, and he will always give
you your answer. Why resist so much, and refuse the
glory of being attached to the body of the faculty ?

BEL. Perhaps she has some other inclination in her
mind.

AN. If I had, Madam, it would be such as reason and
honour would allow.

ARG. Good gracious ! I am acting a pretty part here.

BEL. If I were you, child, I should not force her to
marry ; and I know well enough what I should do.

AN. I am aware, Madam, of what you mean, and of the
kind feelings which you have towards me ; but your designs may not perhaps be so happy as to be executed.

BEL. It is because very circumspect and very respec-
table girls like you, do not care to be obedient and sub-
missive to the wishes of their fathers. That was very well
in times gone by.

AN. The duty of a daughter has its limits, Madam ;
and neither reason nor the laws extend it to other matters.

BEL. This means that your ideas are not averse to marriage ; but that you wish to choose a husband according
to your own fancy.

AN. If my father will not give me a husband whom I
like, I shall beseech him, at least, not to force me to marry one whom I cannot love.

ARG. Gentlemen, I ask your pardon for all this.

AN. Every one has his own motive for marrying. As
for me, who wish no husband but to truly love him, and
who intend to make it a life-long attachment, I confess to
you that I am somewhat cautious about it. There are
some who take husbands only to emancipate themselves
from the restraint of their parents, and to place themselves
in a position to do as they like. There are others, Madam, who make marriage a commerce of sheer interest,
who only wed in order to obtain jointures, to enrich
themselves by the death of those whom they espouse, and
run without scruple from husband to husband, to appro-
priate to themselves their spoils. These persons, in truth
do not stand upon so many ceremonies, and have little
regard to the persons themselves.

BEL. I find you in a great mood for arguing to-day, and I should like to know what you mean by this.

AN. I, Madam? What should I mean but what I say?

BEL. You are so silly, my dear, that there is no enduring you any longer.

AN. You would like to provoke me, Madam, into answering you by some impertinence; but I warn you that you shall not have the advantage.

BEL. Your insolence is matchless.

AN. No, Madam, you may say your best.

BEL. And you have a ridiculous pride, an impertinent presumption, which causes every one to shrug their shoulders.

AN. All this will be of no avail, Madam. I shall be prudent in spite of you; and to take away all hope of your succeeding in what you wish, I shall retire from your presence.

SCENE VIII.—ARGAN, BÈLINE, MR. DIAFOIRUS, THOMAS DIAFOIRUS, TOINETTE.

ARG. (*To Angelique, who is going*). Hark ye. There is no middle way in this case: make up your mind to marry this gentleman in four days, or a convent. (*To Beline*). Do not trouble yourself: I shall manage her properly.

BEL. I am sorry to leave you, child; but I have some business in town which I cannot delay. I shall soon be back again.

ARG. Go, my love, and call in at your notary, that he may attend to what you know.

BEL. Farewell, my little dear.

ARG. Good bye, darling.

SCENE IX.—ARGAN, MR. DIAFOIRUS, THOMAS DIAFOIRUS, TOINETTE.

ARG. There is a woman who loves me . . . it is not to be believed.

MR. D. We are going to take leave of you, Sir.

ARG. Pray, Sir, just tell me in what condition I am.

MR. D. (*Feeling the pulse of Argan*). Come, Thomas, take hold of the other arm of this gentleman, to see whether you can form a good judgment of his pulse. *Quid dicis ?*

THOM. *Dico*, that this gentleman's pulse is the pulse of a man who is not in good health.

MR. D. Good,

THOM. That it is hardish not to say hard.

DR. D. Very well.

THOM. That it acts by fits and starts.

MR. D. *Bene*

THOM. And even a little irregular.

MR. D. *Optime*.

THOM. Which is a sign of intemperature in the *splenetic parenchyma*, which means the milt.

MR. D. Very good.

ARG. No; Mr. Purgon says that it is my liver which is not right.

MR. D. Well, yes: whosoever says *parenchyma*, says the one and the other, on account of the close sympathy there is between them through the *vas breve*, the *pylorus*, and often through the *meatus cholidici*. He no doubt orders you to eat much roast meat.

ARG. No ; nothing but boiled.

MR. D. Well, yes: roast, boiled, the same thing. He prescribes very carefully for you, and you cannot be in better hands.

ARG. Sir, how many grains of salt ought there to be put in an egg?

MR. D. Six, eight, ten, in even numbers, just as in medicine in odd numbers.

ARG. Until we meet again, Sir.

SCENE X.—BÉLINE, ARGAN.

BEL. I have come, child, before going out, to inform you of something to which you ought to look. In passing by Angélique's room, I noticed a young man with her, who ran away the moment he saw me.

ARG. A young man with my daughter !

BEL. Yes. Your little daughter Louison was with them, who can tell you particulars about it.

ARG. Send her here, my love, send her here. Ah! the

bold hussy. (*Alone*). I am no longer astonished at her resistance.

SCENE XI.—ARGAN, LOUISON.

LOU. What do you wish with me, papa? My step-mother has told me that you want me.

ARG. Yes. Come here. Come closer. Turn round. Turn up your eyes. Look at me. Eh?

LOU. What, papa?

ARG. So?

LOU. What?

ARG. Have you nothing to tell me?

LOU. I will tell you, if you like, to amuse you, the story of *The Donkey's Skin*, or the fable of *The Raven and the Fox*, which I have been taught lately.[35]

ARG. That is not what I ask you.

LOU. What then?

ARG. Ah! you' sly girl, you know very well what I mean!

LOU. I beg your pardon, papa.

ARG. Is it thus that you obey me?

LOU. What?

ARG. Did I not recommend you to come and tell me directly all that you see?

LOU. Yes, papa.

ARG. Have you done so?

LOU. Yes, papa. I have come and told you everything I saw.

ARG. And have you seen nothing to-day?

LOU. No, papa.

ARG. No?

LOU. No, papa.

ARG. You are sure?

LOU. I am sure.

ARG. Oh! very well; I shall let you see something.

LOU (*Noticing some switches which Argan has taken up*). Oh! papa.

---

[35] Perrault published the story of *Peru d'Ane* (the Donkey's Skin), in 1694, and as *The Imaginary Invalid* was performed in 1673, it is a proof that it was well known long before it was published.

ARG. Ah! Ah! you little deceiver, you do not tell me that you have seen a man in your sister's room!

LOU. (*Crying*). Papa!

ARG. (*Taking Louison by the arm*). This will teach you to tell lies.

LOU. (*Throwing herself at his knees.*) Ah! papa, I ask your pardon. It is because my sister told me not to tell you; but I am going to tell you all.

ARG. First of all you must be whipped for having told a lie. Afterwards we shall see about the rest.

LOU. Pardon, papa.

ARG. No, no.

LOU. Dear papa, do not whip me.

ARG. You shall be whipped.

LOU. In Heaven's name, papa, do not whip me!

ARG. (*Wanting to whip her*). You shall, you shall.

LOU. Ah! papa, you have hurt me. Wait: I am dead.   (*She pretends to be dead.*

ARG. Hullo! What is this? Louison, Louison! Ah! great Heaven! Louison! Ah! my daughter. Ah! unhappy being that I am! my dear daughter is dead! What have I done, wretch that I am! Ah! these cursed switches! The plague take the switches! Ah! my poor daughter, my poor little Louison!

LOU. There, there, papa do not cry so: I am not entirely dead.

ARG. Do you see the artful little girl! Well, I forgive you this time, provided you really tell me everything.

LOU. Oh! yes, papa.

ARG. You had better be careful in any case; for this little finger knows everything, and will tell me if you tell lies.

LOU. But, papa, do not tell sister that I have told you.

ARG. No, no.

LOU. (*After having made sure that no one is listening*). A man came into sister's room while I was there.

ARG. Well?

LOU. I asked him what he wanted, and he told me that he was her singing-master.

ARG. (*Aside*). Hem, hem! that is it. (*To Louison*). Well?

Lou. Sister came in afterwards.

Arg. Well?

Lou. She said to him: begone, begone, begone. Great Heavens, begone; you will drive me desperate.

Arg. Well?

Lou. And he, he would not go.

Arg. What did he say to her?

Lou. He said to her I do not know how many things.

Arg. And what more?

Lou. He said this, that, and the other, that he loved her dearly, and that she was the prettiest girl in the world.

Arg. And after that?

Lou. And after that, he fell down on his knees before her.

Arg. And after that?

Lou. And after that, he kissed her hands.

Arg. And after that?

Lou. And after that, stepmother came to the door, and he ran away.

Arg. There is nothing else?

Lou. No, papa.

Arg. My little finger, however, mutters something. (*Placing his finger to his ear*). Wait. Eh! ah! ah! Yes? oh! oh! Here is my little finger, which tells me of something that you have seen, but which you have not told me.

Lou. Ah! papa, your little finger is a story-teller.

Arg. Take care.

Lou. No, papa; do not believe it: it tells a story, I assure you.

Arg. Oh! very well, very well, we shall see. Go now, and take notice of everything: go. (*Alone*). Ah! there are no longer any children! Ah! what perplexity! I have not even so much leisure as to think about my illness. Really, I can hold out no longer. (*He drops into a chair.*

SCENE XII.—Béralde, Argan.

Ber. Well, brother! what is the matter? How do you do?

Ar. Ah! brother, very poorly.

BER. How! very poorly?

AR. Yes! I am in so weak a state, that it is incredible.

BER. That is sad.

AR. I have not even the strength to be able to speak.

BER. I came hither, brother, to propose to you a match for my niece Angélique.

AR. (*Speaking excitedly, and rising from his chair*). Brother, do not speak to me about this hussy. She is a wretch, an impertinent, impudent girl, whom I shall place in a convent before two days are over.

BER. Ah! that is right! I am very glad that your strength is coming back a little, and that my visit is doing you good. Well, we will talk of business by-and-by. I have brought you an entertainment with which I fell in, which will dissipate your chagrin, and make you better disposed for what we are to talk about. They are Gipsies dressed as Moors, who perform dances intermixed with songs, with which I am sure you will be pleased ; and this will be as good for you as a prescription of Mr. Purgon. Come.

SECOND INTERLUDE.

The brother of the Imaginary Invalid brings, to amuse him, several Gipsies of both sexes, dressed as Moors, who perform some dances intermixed with music.

1ST MOORISH WOMAN—

> Sweet youth,
> Take advantage of the spring
> Of your best years ;
> Take advantage of the spring
> Of your best years ;
> Abandon yourself to the tender passion.

> Without the amorous flame,
> The most charming pleasures
> Have not sufficient powerful attractions
> To satisfy the heart.

Sweet youth,
Take advantage of the spring
Of your best years;
Abandon yourself to the tender passion.

Do not lose these precious moments,
Beauty vanishes,
Time effaces it;
The age of coldness
Comes in its stead,
Which takes away our taste for these sweet
    pastimes.

Take advantage of the spring
Of your best years,
Sweet youth;
Take advantage of the spring
Of your best years;
Abandon yourself to the tender passion.

First Entry of the Ballet.

Dance of the Gipsies.

2D MOORISH WOMAN—
    What are you thinking of,
    When you press us to love?
    Towards the tender passion
    Our hearts, in our youth,
    Have but too great an inclination.
    Love has, to catch us,
    Such sweet attractions,
    That, from our own will, without waiting,
    We would give ourselves up
    To its first solicitations;
    But all that we hear
    Of the poignant griefs
    And the tears which it costs us,
    Makes us fear
    All its sweetness.

3D MOORISH WOMAN—

> It is sweet, at our age,
> To love tenderly
> A lover
> Who is faithful:
> But, if he be fickle,
> Alas! what torture!

4TH MOORISH WOMAN—

> It is not the unhappiness
> At the lover who breaks his vows;
>> The pain
>> And the rage
> Is that the fickle one
> Keeps possession of our heart.

2D MOORISH WOMAN—

> What part are we to take,
> To defend our young hearts?

3D MOORISH WOMAN—

> Must we deny ourselves to it,
> And flee from its delights.

4TH MOORISH WOMAN—

> Are we to surrender them,
> Notwithstanding their rigours?

TOGETHER—

> Yes, let us abandon ourselves to its ardours,
> Its transports, its whims,
> Its sweet languors,
> If it have some tortures,
> It has a thousand delights
> That charm the heart.

Second Entry of the Ballet.

All the Moors dance together, and make the apes, which they have brought with them perform some jumping.

ACT III.

SCENE I.—BÉRALDE, ARGAN, TOINETTE.

BER. Well! brother, what say you of this? Is it not better than a dose of cassia?

TOI. Humph! good cassia is good.

BER. Well! shall we talk a little together?

ARG. A little patience, brother: I shall be back directly.

TOI. Stay, Sir, you forget that you cannot walk without a stick.

ARG. You are right.

SCENE II.—BÉRALDE, TOINETTE.

TOI. Do not lose sight, if you please, of the interests of your niece.

BER. I shall try everything to obtain for her what she wishes.

TOI. We must absolutely prevent this extravagant match which he has taken into his head; and I have thought to myself that it would be a good thing to introduce into the place a doctor of our own choosing, [36] to disgust him with his Mr. Purgon, and to cry down his treatment of him. But as we have no one at hand to do this, I have made up my mind to play a trick of my own.

BER. How?

TOI. It is a whimsical idea. It may perhaps turn out more lucky than prudent. Let me manage. Act you on your side. There comes our man.

SCENE III.—ARGAN, BÉRALDE.

BER. You will allow me, brother, to ask you, before all things, not to excite yourself in our conversation.

ARG. Agreed.

BER. To reply without bitterness, to the things I may say to you.

ARG. Yes.

BER. And to argue together the matters which we have to discuss, with a mind free from all passion.

---

[36] In the original *un médecin à notre poste.*

ARG. Good Heavens! yes. What a deal of preamble.

BER. Whence comes it, brother, that having the property which you possess, and having no children but one
daughter, for I do not reckon the little one; whence
comes it, I say, that you talk of placing her in a convent?

ARG. Whence comes it brother, that I am master in my
family, to do as I think best?

BER. Your wife does not fail to advise you to get rid,
in that way, of your two daughters, and I have no doubt
that, through a spirit of charity, she would be delighted
to see them both good nuns.

ARG. There now! there we are. There is the poor
woman at once brought up. It is she who does all the
harm, and every one has a grudge against her.

BER. No, brother; let us leave her out of the question.
She is a woman who has the best possible intentions towards your family, and who is devoid of all self-interest;
who has a wonderful tenderness toward you, and who
shows an inconceivable affection and kindness for your
children: that is certain. Let us not speak of that, and
let us go back to your daughter. What is the idea,
brother, of wishing to make her marry the son of a doctor?

ARG. The idea is, of giving myself such a son-in-law as
I want, brother.

BER. This is not your daughter's case, brother; and a
more suitable match offers itself for her.

ARG. Yes; but this one, brother is more suitable to me.

BER. But must the husband she is to take, brother, be
for her, or for you?

ARG. He must be both for her and for me, brother;
and I wish to get into my family the people of whom I
may be in need.

BER. For this reason, if your little girl were grown up,
you would marry her to an apothecary.

ARG. Why not?

BER. Is it possible that you can always be wrapt up in
your apothecaries and your doctors, and that you wish to
be ill in spite of mankind and of nature?

ARG. How do you make that out, brother?

BER. I make it out, brother, that I see no man who is
less ill than you, and that I wish for no better constitution

than your own. A great proof that you are in good health, and that you have a perfectly sound body is, that with all the pains you have taken, you have not been able to succeed as yet in spoiling the goodness of your constitution, and that you are not dead yet with all the physic which they have made you take.

ARG. But do you know, brother, that it is this which preserves me; and that Mr. Purgon says that I should succumb, if he were only three days without taking care of me?

BER. If you do not look to it, he will take so much care of you, that he shall send you into the next world.

ARG. But let us reason a little, brother. You do not believe then in physic?

BER. No, brother, and I do not see that it is necessary to salvation to believe in it.

ARG. What! you do not hold true a matter established throughout the world, and which all ages have reverenced.

BER. Far from holding it true, I consider it, between ourselves, one of the greatest follies of mankind; and to look philosophically at things, I do not see a more amusing mummery; I do not see anything more ridiculous than for one man to undertake to cure another.

ARG. Why cannot you admit, brother, that one man may be able to cure another?

BER. For this reason, brother, that the springs of our machine are a mystery, of which, up to the present, men can see nothing; and that nature has placed too thick a veil before our eyes for our knowing anything about it.

ARG. Then, in your opinion, doctors know nothing?

BER. True, brother, most of them have a deal of classical learning, know how to speak in good Latin, can name all the diseases in Greek, define and classify them; but as regards curing them, that is what they do not know at all.[37]

ARG. But, nevertheless, you must agree that, on this head, doctors know more than other people.

BER. They know, brother, what I have told you, which

---

[37] Béralde's attack on the physicians should be compared with the thirty-seventh chapter of the Second Book of the *Essays* of Montaigne.

does not cure much; and the whole excellence of their art consists in a pompous gibberish, in a specious verbiage, which gives you words instead of reasons, and promises instead of effects.

Arg. But after all, brother, there are people as learned and as clever as you; and we find that, in case of illness, everyone has recourse to doctors.

Ber. It is a sign of human weakness, and not of the truth of their art.

Arg. But doctors must believe in the truth of their art, inasmuch as they make use of it for themselves.

Ber. That is because there are some among them who themselves share in the popular error by which they profit; and others who profit by it without sharing in it. Your Mr. Purgon, for instance, does not discriminate very clearly; he is a thorough physician from head to foot; a man who believes in his rules more than in all mathematical demonstrations, and who would think it a crime to wish to examine them; who sees nothing obscure in physic, nothing dubious, nothing difficult, and who, with an impetuosity of prejudice, a stiff-necked assurance, a coarse common sense and reasoning, rushes into purging and bleeding, and hesitates at nothing. You must not owe him a grudge for all he might do to you: he would despatch you with the most implicit faith; and he would, in killing you, only do what he has done to his wife and children, and what, if there were any need, he would do to himself.

Arg. That is because you bear him a grudge from infancy, brother.[38] But to cut it short, let us come to the fact. What must we do, then, when we are ill?

Ber. Nothing, brother.

Arg. Nothing?

Ber. Nothing. We must remain quiet. If we leave nature alone, she recovers gently from the disorder into which she has fallen. It is our anxiety, our impatience, which spoils all; and nearly all men die of their remedies, not of their diseases.

Arg. But you must admit, brother, that this nature may be assisted by certain things.

---

[38] The original has *vous avez, mon frère, une dent de lait contre lui; dent de lait* means literally, a first or shedding tooth.

BER. Good Heavens! brother, these are mere ideas with which we love to beguile ourselves; and, at all times, beautiful fictions have crept in amongst men, in which we believe, because they flatter us, and because it were to be wished that they were true. When a physician speaks to you of aiding, assisting, and supporting nature, to take away from her what is hurtful, and to give her that which she wants, to re-establish her, and to put her in the full possession of her functions; when he speaks to you of rectifying the blood, of regulating the bowels and the brain, of relieving the spleen, of putting the chest to rights, of mending the liver, of strengthening the heart, of renewing and preserving the natural heat, and of being possessed of secrets to prolong life till an advanced age, he just tells you the romance of physic. But when you come to the truth and experience, you find nothing of all this; and it is like those beautiful dreams, which, on awaking, leave you nothing but the regret of having believed in them.

ARG. Which means that all the knowledge of the world is contained in your head, and that you profess to know more about it than all the great physicians of our age.

BER. In speaking and in reality, your great physicians are two different sorts of persons. Hear them hold forth, they are the cleverest people in the world; see them act, they are the most ignorant of all men.

ARG. Lack-a-day! you are a great doctor; and I should much like to have one of these gentlemen here, to refute your arguments, and to take you down a peg or two.

BER. I, brother, I do not assume the task of combating the Faculty; and every one, at his own risk and cost, may believe whatever he pleases. What I say about it is simply between ourselves, and I should have wished to be somewhat able to dispel the error in which you are, and to take you, for your amusement, to see one of the comedies of Molière upon this subject.

ARG. Your Molière, with his comedies, is a fine impertinent fellow! and I think it is like his impudence to go and bring upon the stage such worthy persons as the physicians.

BER. He does not make fun of physicians, but of the ridiculousness of physic.

Arg. It is like him to do so, to interfere about controlling the Faculty ! There is a fine booby, a brazen impertinent fellow, to make fun of consultations and prescriptions, to attack the body of physicians, and to put on his stage such venerable persons as these gentlemen !

Ber. What would you have him put there but the various professions of men? They put princes and kings there every day, who are of quite as good family as physicians.

Arg. Now, by all that is terrible !³⁹ if I were the physicians, I would avenge myself of his impertinence; and would let him die without assistance, whenever he felt ill. He might say and do what he liked; I would not prescribe even the least bleeding, or the smallest enema; and I would say to him: die, die; that will teach you another time to make fun of the Faculty.

Ber. You are very angry with him?

Arg. Yes. He is a foolish fellow ; and if the physicians be wise, they will do what I say.

Ber. He will be wiser still than your physicians, for he will not ask them for their assistance.

Arg. So much the worse for him, if he have no recourse to remedies.

Ber. He has his reasons for not wishing for them, and he maintains that it is permitted only to robust and vigorous people, who have sufficient strength left to bear the remedies with the disease ; but that, as for him, he has just strength enough to bear his illness.

Arg. Silly reasons these ! There, brother, let us talk no more about this man ; for he excites my bile, and you will bring on my illness again.

Ber. Very well, brother ; and to change our conversation, I will tell you, that on account of a trifling repugnance on the part of your daughter, you should not take the violent resolution to place her in a convent : that in the choice of a son-in-law, you should not blindly yield to a passion which carries you away; and that, in such a matter, you should accommodate yourself somewhat to

---

³⁹ The original has *Par la mort non de diable*, used for *Par la mort de Dieu, non, de diable!*

the inclination of your child, seeing that it is for her life, and that on it depends the happiness of a union.

SCENE IV.—MR. FLEURANT, *carrying a syringe;* ARGAN, BÉRALDE.

ARG. Ah! by your leave, brother.

BER. What are you going to do?

ARG. Take this little enema: it will soon be done.

BER. You are jesting. Cannot you be a moment without an enema or some physic? Put it off till another time, and remain quiet a little.

ARG. It will be for to-night or for to-morrow morning, Mr. Fleurant.

MR. F. (*To Béralde*). With what do you meddle, to oppose the prescription of the Faculty, and to prevent this gentleman from taking my enema? It is very ridiculous of you to be so rash!

BER. Begone, Sir; we see well enough that you are not accustomed to speak to people's faces.

MR. F. One should not thus make fun of physic, and make me waste my time. I have come here only with a good prescription; and I shall go and tell Mr. Purgon how I have been prevented from executing his orders, and from performing my function. You shall see, you shall see . . .

SCENE V.—ARGAN, BÉRALDE.

ARG. You will be the cause of some mishap here, brother.

BER. A great mishap not to take an enema which Mr. Purgon has ordered! Once more, brother, is it possible that there is no way of curing you of that mania for physicians, and that you wish to be buried all the days of your life in their remedies?

ARG. Good Heavens! brother, you talk of it as a man who is in perfect health; but if you were in my place, you would soon change your language. It is easy to talk against physic, when one is in good health.

BER. But what illness have you?

ARG. You will drive me mad. I wish you had it, my

illness, just to see whether you would prate so much.   Ah !
here comes Mr. Purgon.

SCENE VI.—MR. PURGON, ARGAN, BÉRALDE, TOINETTE.

MR. P. I have just heard some pretty news at the door ;
that people are making jest of my prescriptions here, and
refuse to take the remedies which I have prescribed.

ARG. Sir, it is not . . .

MR. P. This is a very rash proceeding, a strange revolt
of a patient against his physician.

TOI. This is horrible,

MR. P. An enema which I had taken a pleasure in
compounding myself.

ARG. It is not I . . .

MR. P. Invented and concocted according to all the
rules of the art.

TOI. He is wrong.

MR. P. And which was to produce a marvellous effect on
the bowels.

ARG. My brother . . .

MR. P. To send it back with contempt !

ARG. (*Pointing to Bèralde*). It is he . . . .

MR. P. It is a most daring deed.

TOI. That is true.

MR. P. An enormous outrage against the medical profession.

ARG. (*Pointing to Béralde*). He is the cause . . .

MR. P. A crime of high treason against the Faculty,
which cannot be sufficiently punished.

TOI. You are right.

MR. P. I declare that I break off all connection with
you.

ARG. It is my brother . . .

MR. P. That I no longer desire an alliance with you.

TOI. You will do well.

MR. P. And that to make an end of all union with
you, there is the deed of gift which I made to my nephew,
in favour of the marriage. (*He tears the document to
pieces, and throws the pieces furiously about.*

ARG. It is my brother who has done all the harm.

MR. P. To despise my enema!

ARG. Let it be brought ; I will take it.

MR. P. I would have cured you before long.

TOI. He does not deserve it.

MR. P. I was going to cleanse your body, and drive out all the bad humours.

ARG. Ah! brother!

MR. P. And it wanted but a dozen more medicines to cure you completely.

TOI. He is unworthy of your care.

MR. P. But as you do not wish to be cured by my hands . . .

ARG. It is not my fault.

MR. P. Since you have withdrawn from the obedience which a man owes to his physician . . .

TOI. That cries for vengeance.

MR. P. Since you have declared yourself a rebel against the remedies which I prescribed for you . . .

ARG. Eh, not at all.

MR. P. I must tell you that I give you up to your bad constitution, to the intemperate of your bowels, to the corruption of your blood, to the acrimony of your bile, and to the feculence of your humours.

TOI. That is very well done.

ARG. Oh, Heavens!

MR. P. And I will that in four days you shall be in an incurable state.

ARG. Ah, mercy!

MR. P. That you fall into a bradypepsia.

ARG. Mr. Purgon!

MR. P. From bradypepsia into dyspepsia.

ARG. Mr. Purgon!

MR. P. From dyspepsia into apepsy.

ARG. Mr. Purgon!

MR. P. From apepsy into lientery.

ARG. Mr. Purgon!

MR. P. From lientery into dysentery.

ARG. Mr. Purgon!

MR. P. From dysentery into dropsy.

ARG. Mr. Purgon!

Mr. P. And from dropsy into a privation of life, whither your folly will lead you.[40]

Scene VII.—Argan, Béralde.

Arg. Ah, Heavens! I am dead. Brother, you have undone me.

Ber. Why! what is the matter?

Arg. I can hold out no longer. I already feel the vengeance of the faculty.

Ber. Really, brother, you are mad; and I would not have people see you act as you do, for a great deal. Just bear up a little, I pray; be yourself, and do not give way so much to your imagination.

Arg. You see, brother, the strange diseases with which he has threatened me.

Ber. What a simpleton you are!

Arg. He says that I shall become incurable before four days are over.

Ber. What does it signify what he says? Is it an oracle that has spoken? To hear you speak, it looks as if Mr. Purgon holds in his hands the thread of your life, and that by a supreme authority he lengthens or shortens it for you, as it pleases him. Remember that the springs of your existence are in yourself, and that the wrath of Mr. Purgon is as little capable of killing you as his remedies are of keeping you alive. Here is an opportunity, if you wish, to rid yourself of the physicians; or if you were born so as not to be able to do without them, it is easy to have another with whom, brother, you may run a little less risk.

Arg. Ah! brother, he knows my entire constitution, and the way how to treat me.

Ber. I must confess to you that you are a man of great prejudice, and that you look at matters with strange eyes.

Scene VIII.—Argan, Béralde, Toinette.

Toi. (To Argan). Sir, here is a doctor who wishes to see you.

---

[40] Bradypepsia is a slow and imperfect digestion; apepsy is a defective digestion; lientery is a diarrhœa, in which the food is discharged only half digested.

ARG. And what doctor?

TOI. A doctor of the Faculty.

ARG. I ask you who he is.

TOI. I do not know him, but he is as like me as two drops of water; and if I were not sure that my mother was an honest woman, I should say that this was some little brother which she has given me since my father's death.

ARG. Let him come in.

SCENE IX.—ARGAN, BÉRALDE.

BER. You are served according to your wish. One physician leaves you; another presents himself.

ARG. I greatly fear that you may be the cause of some mishap.

BER. Again! You will always harp upon this.

ARG. But look you! All these diseases of which I know nothing weigh on my mind; these . . .

SCENE X.—ARGAN, BÉRALDE, TOINETTE, *disguised as a physician.*

TOI. Permit me to pay you this visit, Sir, and to offer you my small services for all the bleedings and purgings of which you may be in want.

ARG. Sir, I am much obliged to you. (*To Béralde*). Upon my word, this is Toinette himself.

TOI. Pray, excuse me, Sir; I have forgotten to give a message to my servant; I shall be back immediately.

SCENE XI.—ARGAN, BÉRALDE.

ARG. Eh? would you not swear that it was really Toinette?

BER. It is true that the likeness is very great indeed; but it is not the first time that we have seen this kind of things; and history is full of these freaks of nature.

ARG. As for me, I am amazed at it; and . . .

SCENE XII.—ARGAN, BÉRALDE, TOINETTE.[41]

TOI. What do you want, Sir?

---

[41] "Toinette has doffed her physician's dress so soon that it is difficult to believe that she appeared as a doctor before." This note is in the edition of Molière's works of 1682.

ARG. How?

TOI. Did not you call me?

ARG. I? no.

TOI. My ears must have tingled then.

ARG. Just remain here a moment, to see how this phyiscian resembles you.

TOI. (*Going out*). Yes, indeed! I have business elsewhere; and I have seen him enough.

SCENE XIII.—ARGAN, BÉRALDE.

ARG. If I had not seen them both, I should have believed it was but one.

BER. I have read of surprising instances of these kinds of likenesses; and we have seen some of them, in our own times, by which the whole world has been deceived.

ARG. As for me, I should have been deceived by this one; and I should have sworn that it was the same person.

SCENE XIV.—ARGAN, BÉRALDE; TOINETTE, *as a physician*.

TOI. Sir, I ask your pardon with all my heart.

ARG. (*Softly to Béralde*). This is wonderful.

TOI. You will not take amiss, pray, the curiosity which I had to see such an illustrious patient as you; and your reputation, which has spread everywhere, may excuse the liberty which I have taken.

ARG. I am your servant, Sir.

TOI. I perceive, Sir, that you are looking earnestly at me. How old do you really think I am?

ARG. I think that you may be six or seven and twenty at the most.

TOI. Ha, ha, ha, ha, ha! I am ninety.

ARG. Ninety!

TOI. Yes. You observe an effect of the secrets of my art, to keep myself so fresh and vigorous.

ARG. Upon my word, this is a fine youthful old man for ninety!

TOI. I am an itinerant physician who go from town to town, from province to province, from kingdom to kingdom, in search of illustrious materials for my art, to find patients worthy of my attention, capable of having applied to them the grand and beautiful secrets which I have discovered in medicine.   I disdain to amuse myself with these small fry of ordinary complaints, with trifling rheumatisms and colds, small agues, vapours, and head-aches.   I want diseases of importance, real non-intermit-tent fevers, with a disordered brain, real purple fevers, real plagues, real confirmed dropsies, real pleurisies with inflammations of the lungs ; these are what please me ; that is where I triumph ; and I wish, Sir, that you had been given up by all the physicians, despaired of, at the point of death, that I might show you the excellence of my remedies, and the desire which I have to be of service to you.

ARG. I am obliged to you, Sir, for the kindness you have for me.

TOI. Let me feel your pulse.   Come, beat as you should.   Ah! I shall make you go as you ought.   Ho! this pulse plays the impertinent ; I perceive well enough that you do not know me as yet.   Who is your physician ?

ARG. Mr. Purgon.

TOI. This man is not in my note-book amongst the great physicians.   From what does he say that you suffer ?

ARG. He says it is from the liver, and others say it is from the spleen.

TOI. They are all blockheads.   It is from the lungs that you are ill.

ARG. From the lungs?

TOI. Yes.   What do you feel ?

ARG. I feel from time to time qualms.

TOI. Exactly, the lungs.

ARG. I seem to have a mist before my eyes some-times.

TOI. The lungs.

ARG. I have now and then a pain at the heart.

TOI. The lungs.

ARG. I feel a weariness in my limbs at times.

TOI. The lungs.

ARG. And now and then I am taken with pains in the stomach, just as if it were the colics.

TOI. The lungs.   Do you relish your food ?

ARG. Yes, Sir.

TOI. The lungs. You like to take a little wine?

ARG. Yes, Sir.

TOI. The lungs. You feel an inclination to take a little nap after your meals, and you are glad to go to sleep?

ARG. Yes, Sir.

TOI. The lungs, the lungs, I tell you. What does the doctor order you to eat?

ARG. He orders me soup.

TOI. The ignorant fellow!

ARG. Poultry.

TOI. The ignorant fellow!

ARG. Veal.

TOI. The ignorant fellow!

ARG. Broth.

TOI. The ignorant fellow!

ARG. New-laid eggs.

TOI. The ignorant fellow!

ARG. And in the evening some prunes to loosen the belly.

TOI. The ignorant fellow!

ARG. And above all, to take my wine well diluted.

TOI. *Ignorantus*, *ignoranta*, *ignorantum*. You must drink your wine pure, and, to thicken your blood, which is too thin, you must eat good solid beef, good solid pork, good Dutch cheese; groats and rice, and chestnuts and thin cakes, to thicken and conglutinate. Your doctor is an ass. I shall send you one of my choice; and I shall come to see you from time to time, while I am in this town.

ARG. You will oblige me very much.

TOI. What the deuce do you want with this arm?

ARG. How?

TOI. I would have this arm cut off instanter if I were you.

ARG. And why?

TOI. Do you not see that it attracts to itself all the nourishment, and that it prevents this side from growing.

ARG. Yes; but I want my arm.

TOI. You have a right eye there, too, which I would have taken out, if I were in your place.

ARG. An eye taken out?

TOI. Do you not see that it incommodes the other, and robs it of its nourishment? Believe me, have it taken out as quickly as possible; you will see all the clearer with the left eye.

ARG. There is no hurry.

TOI. Farewell. I am sorry to leave you so soon; but I must be present at a great consultation which is to be held about a man who died yesterday.

ARG. About a man who died yesterday?.

TOI. Yes: to consider and see what ought to have been done to cure him. Until we meet again.

ARG. You know that invalids are excused from seeing any one to the door.

SCENE XV.—ARGAN, BÉRALDE.

BER. This physician really seems very clever.

ARG. Yes; but he does things a little too quickly.

BER. All great physicians are like that.

ARG. To cut off an arm, to take out an eye, so that the other may be better! I much prefer that the other should not be quite so well. A fine operation, to make me one-eyed and one-armed.

SCENE XVI.—ARGAN, BÉRALDE, TOINETTE.

TOI. (*Pretending to speak to some one outside*). Come, come, I am your humble servant, I am in no mood to be merry.

ARG What is the matter?

TOI. Your physician, troth who wished to feel my pulse.

ARG. Look at that, at the age of ninety.

BER. Well now! brother, since your Mr. Purgon has fallen out with you, will you not give me leave to speak to you about the match which is proposed for my niece.

ARG. No, brother: I mean to place her in a convent, for having run counter to my wishes. I perceive well enough that there is some love-affair in the case; and I discovered a certain secret interview which they do not know that I have discovered.

BER. Well! brother; and suppose there is some slight

inclination, would that be so very criminal? And can there be aught in it to offend you, when all this aims only at what is honourable, marriage.

ARG. Be that as it may, brother, she shall be a nun; that is a settled thing.

BER. You wish to please some one.

ARG. I understand you. You always come back to that, and you dislike my wife.

BER Well then! yes, brother: since I am to speak frankly to you, it is your wife I am alluding to; and I can no more bear your infatuation for physic, than your infatuation for her, and see you running headlong into all the snares which she spreads for you.

TOI. Ah! Sir, do not talk about my mistress; she is a woman of whom nothing can be said, a woman without any guile, and who loves my master, who loves him . . . One cannot express it.

ARG. Just ask her how she caresses me.

TOI. That is true.

ARG. What uneasiness my illness causes her.

TOI. Assuredly.

ARG. And the care and the pains she takes about me.

TOI. To be sure. (*To Béralde*). Do you wish me to convince you, and to show you immediately how my mistress loves master? (*To Argan*). Allow me to show him his blunder, Sir, and to convince him of his error.[42]

ARG. How?

TOI. The mistress is coming back. Put yourself at full length in this chair, and pretend that you are dead. You shall see the grief she shall be in, when I tell her the news.

ARG. I will do it.

TOI. Yes; but do not leave her long in despair; for she might die of it.

ARG. Leave it to me.

TOI. (*To Béralde*). And you, hide yourself in this corner.

SCENE XVII.—ARGAN, BÉRALDE.

ARG. Is there not some danger in counterfeiting death?

---

[42] The original has *souffrez que je lui montre son bec-jaune*. See Vol. II., *Don Juan*, page 101, note 11.

TOI. No, no. What danger should there be? Only stretch yourself out there. (*Softly*). It will be a pleasure to confound your brother. Here comes the mistress. Steady as you are.

SCENE XVIII.—BÉLINE, ARGAN, *stretched out in his chair;* TOINETTE.

TOI. (*Pretending not to see Béline*). Ah! good Heavens! Ah! what a misfortune! What a strange accident!

BEL. What ails you, Toinette?

TOI. Ah! mistress!

BEL. What is the matter?

TOI. Your husband is dead.

BEL. My husband is dead?

TOI. Alas! yes! the poor man is gone.

BEL. Are you sure?

TOI. I am sure. No one knows the accident as yet; and I was here all alone. He just now passed away in my arms. Look, there he is at full length in his chair.

BEL. Heaven be praised for it! I have got rid of a great burden. How silly you are, Toinette, to make yourself miserable about this death!

TOI. I thought, mistress, that I ought to cry.

BEL. Come, come, it is not worth while. What do we lose in him; and what good was he upon the earth? A man who was a trouble to everybody, dirty, disgusting, never without some enema or physic in him, always blowing his nose, coughing or spitting; without sense, tiresome, bad-tempered, for ever fatiguing people, and scolding night and day the maids and the servants.

TOI. This is a pretty funeral oration!

BEL. You must help me, Toinette, to execute my plan; and you may depend upon it that, in helping me, your reward shall be sure. Since, by good fortune, no one has as yet been told of the affair, let us carry him to his bed, and keep his death secret, until I have managed my business. There are some papers, there is some money which I wish to get hold of; and it would not be just that I should have fruitlessly wasted the prime of my years with him. Come, Toinette; let us first of all take his keys.

ARG. (*Suddenly getting up*). Gently.

BEL. Oh !

ARG. Aha ! my lady, that is how you love me !

TOI. Ah ! Ah ! the dead man is not dead.

ARG. (*To Béline, who is going*).   I am very glad to see your good feeling, and to have heard the fine panegyric which you have pronounced on me.   This is a wholesome advice which will make me more prudent for the future, and which will prevent me from doing many things.[43]

SCENE XIX.—BÉRALDE, *coming out of the corner where he has been hidden;* ARGAN, TOINETTE.

BER. Well, brother, you see now ?

TOI. Upon my word, I should never have believed this. But I hear your daughter.   Place yourself again as you were, and let us see in what manner she will take your death.   It is not a bad thing to find out ; and, while you are about it, you shall know, by these means, the feelings of your family for you.

(*Béralde goes into hiding again.*)

SCENE XX.—ARGAN, ANGÉLIQUE, TOINETTE.

TOI. (*Pretending not to see Angélique*). Oh, Heaven ! Ah, sad event ! Unhappy day !

AN. What ails you Toinette ? and why do you cry ?

TOI. Alas ! I have sad news to tell you.

AN. Eh ! what ?

TOI. Your father is dead.

AN. My father is dead, Toinette ?

TOI. Yes.   There he is.   He has just died of a fainting fit that took him.

AN. Oh, Heaven ! what a misfortune ! what a cruel blow ! Alas ! am I to lose my father, the only thing I had left in the world ; and, still more, to complete my unhappiness, must I lose him in a moment when he was angry with me ! What is to become of me, unhappy being? and what consolation shall I find after so great a loss ?

---

[43] The primary idea of the character of Béline is to be found in a farce, played before Molière came to Paris, and called *The Sick Husband ;*—wherein a wife rejoices, with her lover, on hearing of the death of her spouse.

SCENE XXI.—ARGAN, ANGÉLIQUE, CLÉANTE, TOINETTE.

CLE. What is the matter, fair Angelique? and what misfortune are you bewailing?

AN. Alas! I am bewailing all that I could lose of what is most dear and precious in life; I am bewailing the death of my father.

CLE. Oh, Heavens! what an accident! what an unforeseen blow. Alas! after the request for your hand which I besought your uncle to make for me, I came to introduce myself to him, and to try, by my respects and entreaties, to dispose his heart to grant you to my love.

AN. Ah! Cléante! let us no longer talk of anything; let us leave all thoughts of marriage. After the loss of my father, I will no longer belong to this world, and I renounce it forever. Yes, father, if I have just now opposed your inclinations, I shall at least carry out one of your intentions, and make amends, by that, for the grief which I accuse myself of having caused you. (*Throwing herself at his feet*). Suffer me, father, now to pledge you my word, and to embrace you, to show you my repentance.

ARG. (*Embracing Angélique*). Ah! daughter.

AN. Oh!

ARG. Come. Have no fear; I am not dead. There, you are my own flesh and blood, my own dear daughter; and I am delighted to have seen your good feeling.

SCENE XXII.—ARGAN, TOINETTE, ANGÉLIQUE, CLÉANTE, BÉRALDE.

AN. Ah! what an agreeable surprise! Father, since, by an extreme good fortune, Heaven has given you back to my love, suffer me to throw myself at your feet to beseech you for one thing. If you are not favourable to the inclination of my heart; if you refuse me Cléante for a husband, I implore you, at least, not to force me to marry another. This is all the favour I ask of you.

CLE. (*Throwing himself at Argan's feet*). Oh! Sir, allow yourself to be touched by her prayers and mine; and do not show yourself opposed to the mutual ardour of such a fine affection.

BER. Can you still hold out, brother?

Toi. Can you be insensible to so much love, Sir?

Arg. Let him become a doctor, and I consent to the marriage. (*To Cléante*). Yes, become a physician, and I give you my daughter.

Cle. With all my heart, Sir. If it depends but upon this to be your son-in-law, I shall become a doctor, an apothecary even, if you wish it. It is not much to do, and I would consent to many other things to obtain the fair Angélique.

Ber. But, brother, a thought comes into my head. Become a physician yourself. The convenience will be still greater of having within yourself all that you need.

Toi. That is true. That is the proper way of getting quickly cured ; and there is no complaint so daring as to meddle with the person of a physician.

Arg. I think that you are jesting with me, brother. Am I of an age to study?

Ber. To study! that is good. You are learned enough; and there are many among them, who are not more clever than you are.

Arg. But one should know to speak Latin well, understand the diseases, and the remedies to apply.

Ber. In receiving the gown and the cap of a physician, you will learn all that; and you will afterwards be more skilful than you like to be.

Arg. What! do people know how to discourse upon diseases when they have on that gown?

Ber. Yes. You have but to speak with a gown and a cap, and any gibberish becomes learned, and all nonsense becomes sense.

Toi. There, Sir, if it was only for your beard, that goes a great way already ; for the beard makes more than half of the physician.

Cle. In any case, I am ready to do everything.

Ber. Will you have the thing done immediately?

Arg. How, immediately?

Ber. Yes, and in your own house.

Arg. In my own house?

Ber. Yes. I know a body of physicians, friends of mine, who will come instantly and perform the ceremony in your hall. It will cost you nothing.

ARG. But I, what am I to say? what to answer?

BER. You will be instructed in two words, and they will give you in writing what you are to say. Go and put on a decent dress. I shall go and fetch them.

ARG. Well, let us see all this.

SCENE XXIII.—BÉRALDE, ANGÉLIQUE, CLÉANTE, TOINETTE.

CLE. What do you mean? and what do you understand by these physician friends of yours?

TOI. What is your plan, then?

BER. To amuse ourselves a little this evening. The comedians have composed a slight interlude about the installation of a physician with music and dances. I wish that we should enjoy the entertainment together, and that my brother should play the principal personage in it.

AN. But, uncle, I think that you are jesting a little too much with my father.

BER. But, niece, it is rather accommodating ourselves to his whims than jesting with him. All this is only between ourselves. We can each of us take a part in it ourselves, and thus perform the comedy for one another. The carnival authorizes all this. Come, let us quickly go and get everything ready.

CLE. (*To Angélique*). Do you consent?

AN. Yes, since my uncle manages the affair.

THIRD INTERLUDE.

A Burlesque Ceremony of admitting a Doctor of Medicine in recitative Music and Dancing.

Several upholsterers enter to prepare the hall, and place the benches to music. After which the whole assembly, composed of eight syringe-bearers, six apothecaries, twenty-two doctors, and the person that is to be admitted physician, eight surgeons dancing, and two singing, enter, and take their places, each according to his rank.

PRAESES.   Savantissimi Doctores,[44]
                Medicinæ Professores,
                Qui hic assemblati estis ;
                Et vos, altri messiores,
                Sententiarum Facultatis
                Fideles executores ;
                Chirurgiani et apothecari,
                Atque tota compania aussi,
                Salus, honor, et argentum,
                Atque bonum appetitum.

                Non possum, docti confreri
                En moi satis admirari,
                Qualis bona inventio,
                Est medici professio ;
Quam bella chosa est et benè trovata,
                Medicina illa benedicta,
                Quæ, suo nomine solo,
                Surprenanti miraculo,
                Depuis si longo tempore,
                Facit à gogo vivere
                Tant de gens omni genere.

                Per totam terrum videmus
                Grandam vogam ubi sumus ;
                Et quods grandes et petiti
                Sunt de nobis infatuti.
Totus mundus, currens ad nostros remedios,
                Nos regardat sicut deos,
                Et nostris ordonnanciis
Principes et Reges soumissos videtis.

                Doncque il est nostræ sapientiæ,
                Boni sensus atque prudentiæ,
                De fortement travaillare
                A nos bene conservare
                In tali credito, voga et honore ;

---

[44] In this interlude there is such an amount of Latin, dog-Latin, Italian, French, and of words belonging to no language under the sun, that, by rendering any of it into English, the effect of the whole is greatly marred. I have, therefore, left it in the original.

Et prendere gardam à non recevere
    In nostro docto corpore,
    Quam personas capabiles,
    Et totas dignas remplire
    Has plaças honorabiles.
C'est pour cela que nunc convocatis estis;
    Et credo quod trovabitis
    Dignam matieram medici
    In savanti homine que voici;
    Lequel, in chosis omnibus;
    Dono ad interrogandum,
    Et à fond examinandum
    Vostris capacitatibus.

PRIMUS DOCTOR.

    Si mihi licentiam dat dominus praeses,
      Et tanti docti doctores,
      Et assistantes illustres,
      Très-savanti bacheliero,
      Quem estimo honoro,
    Domandabo causam et rationem quare
      Opium facit dormire.

BACHELIERUS.

      Mihi à docto doctore.
    Domandatur causam et rationem quare
      Opium facit domire.
      A quoi respondeo;
      Quia est in eo
      Virtus dormitiva,
      Cujus est natura
      Sensus assoupire. [45]

CHORUS. Bene, bene, bene respondere.
      Dignus, dignus est intrare
      In nostro docto corpore.
      Bene, bene respondere.

---

[45] In Descartes' time, and before him, everything was explained by forms, virtues, entities, quiddities. A thing was cold because it had a frigorific virtue; hot because it had a calorific virtue.

SECUNDUS DOCTOR.
  Cum permissione domini præsidis
          Doctissimæ Facultatis,
          Et totius his nostris actis
          Companiæ assistantis,
  Domandabo tibi, docte bacheliere,
          Quæ sunt remedia
          Quæ, in maladia
          Dite hydropisia
          Convenit facere?

BACHELIERUS.
          Clysterium donare,
          Postea seignare,
          Ensuita purgare.

CHORUS. Bene, bene, bene, bene respondere
          Dignus, dignus, est intrare
          In nostros docto corpore.

TERTIUS DOCTOR.
  Si bonum semblatur domino præsidi,
          Doctissimæ Facultati,
          Et companiæ præsenti,
  Domandabo tibi, docte bacheliere,
          Quæ remedia eticis,
          Pulmonicis atque asmaticis
          Trovas à propos facere.

BACHELIERUS.
          Clysterium donare,
          Postea seignare,
          Ensuita purgare.

CHORUS. Bene, bene, bene respondere.
          Dignus, dignus est intrare
          In nostro docto corpore.

QUARTUS DOCTOR.
          Super illas maladias,
  Doctus bachelierus dixit maravillas;
  Mais, si non ennuyo dominum præsidem,
          Doctissimam Facultatem,
          Et totam honorabilem
          Companiam ecoutantem;

Faciam illi unam questionem.
Dès hiero maladus unus
Tombavit in meas manus;
Habet grandam fievram cum redoublamentis,
Grandam dolorem capitis,
Et grandum malum au côté.
Cum granda difficultate
Et pena de respirare.
Veillas mihi dire,
Docte bacheliere
Quid illi facere.

BACHELIERUS.

Clysterium donare,
Postea seignare,
Ensuita purgare.

QUINTUS DOCTOR.

Mais, si maladia
Opiniatria
Non vult se garire,
Quid illi facere?

BACHELIERUS. Clysterium donare
Postea seignare,
Ensuita purgare..
Reseignare, repurgare, et reclysterisare.

CHORUS. Bene, bene, bene, bene respondere:
Dignus, dignus est intrare
In nostro docto corpore.

PRAESES. Juras gardare statuta
Per Facultatem præscripta,
Cum sensu et jugeamento?

BACHELIERUS. Juro.[46]

---

[46] It is said that Molière felt so ill on pronouncing these words, at the fourth representation of *The Imaginary Invalid*, that he could not get on any longer, and the curtain was obliged to fall.

PRAESES.   Essere in omnibus
                    Consultationibus,
                    Ancieni aviso,
                    Aut bono,
                    Aut mauvaiso?

BACHELIERUS.   Juro.

PRAESES.   De non jamais te servire
                    De remediis aucunis,
                    Quam de ceux seulement doctæ Facultatis,
                    Maladus dût-il crevare
                    Et mori de suo malo?

BACHELIERUS.   Juro.

PRAESES.   Ego, cum isto boneto
                    Venerabili et docto,
                    Dono tibi et concedo
                    Virtutem et puissanciam
                            Medicandi,
                            Purgandi,
                            Seignandi,
                            Perçandi,
                            Taillandi,
                            Coupandi,
                            Et occidendi
                Impune per totam terram.

Entry of the Ballet.

*All the Surgeons and Apothecaries come to do him reverence
to Music.*

BACH.   Grandes doctores doctrinæ
                    De la rhubarbe et du séné,
            Ce serait sans douta à moi chosa folla,
                    Inepta et ridicula,
                    Si j'alloibam m' engageare
                    Vobis louangeas donare,
                    Et entreprenoibam adjoutare
                    Des lumieras au soleïllo,
                    Et des etoilas au cielo,
                    Des ondas á l' Oceano;
                    Et des rosas au printano.

Agreate qu' avec uno moto
Pro toto remercimento
Rendam gratias corpori tam docto.
Vobis, vobis debeo
Bien plus qu' à naturæ et qu' à patri meo.
Natura et pater meus
Hominem me habent factum ;
Mais vos me, ce qui est bien plus,
Avetis factum medicum :
Honor, favor et gratia,
Qui, in hoc corde que voilà,
Imprimant ressentimenta
Qui dureront in secula.

CHORUS.   Vivat, vivat, vivat, vivat, cent fois vivat
                Novus doctor, qui tam bene parlat !
           Mille, mille annis, et manget et bibat,
                Et seignet et tuat !

Third Entry of the Ballet.

*All the Surgeons and Apothecaries dance to the sound of the
Instruments and Voices, and clapping of hands, and
Apothecaries' Mortars.*

Chirurgus. Puisse-t-il voir doctas
            Suas ordonnancias,
            Omnium chirurgorum,
            Et apothicarum
            Remplire boutiquas !

Chorus. Vivat, vivat, vivat, vivat, cent fois vivat,
          Novus doctor, qui, tam bene parlat
        Mille, mille annis, et manget et bibat,
          Et seignet et tuat !

Chirurgus. Puissent toti anni
            Lui essere boni
            Et favorabiles,
            Et n' habere jamais
            Quam pestas, verolas,
            Fievras, pleuresias
            Fluxus de sang et dyssenterias !

Chorus. Vivat, vivat, vivat, vivat, cent fois vivat,
            Novus doctor, qui tam bene parlat !
            Mille, mille annis, et magnet et bibat,
            Et seignet et tuat !

*The Doctors, Surgeons and Apothecaries go out all according
to their several ranks, with the same ceremony as they
entered.*[47]

---

[47] There exists also an addition to the ceremony, namely, speeches of
three other doctors, and some variations in those of the physicians who
have spoken, as well as in other parts of the ceremony.   But as these
changes are found only in the editions of Rouen and Amsterdam, and are
most probably not by Molière, we do not give them here.